GRACE PARKER'S PEACH PIE

KAY CORRELL

ZURA LU PUBLISHING LLC

KAY'S BOOKS

Find more information on all my books at
kaycorrell.com

COMFORT CROSSING ~ THE SERIES

The Shop on Main - Book One

The Memory Box - Book Two

The Christmas Cottage - A Holiday Novella
(Book 2.5)

The Letter - Book Three

The Christmas Scarf - A Holiday Novella
(Book 3.5)

The Magnolia Cafe - Book Four

The Unexpected Wedding - Book Five

The Wedding in the Grove - (a crossover short

story between series - with Josephine and Paul from The Letter.)

LIGHTHOUSE POINT ~ THE SERIES
Wish Upon a Shell - Book One
Wedding on the Beach - Book Two
Love at the Lighthouse - Book Three
Cottage near the Point - Book Four
Return to the Island - Book Five
Bungalow by the Bay - Book Six

CHARMING INN ~ Return to Lighthouse Point
One Simple Wish - Book One
Two of a Kind - Book Two
Three Little Things - Book Three
Four Short Weeks - Book Four
Five Years or So - Book Five
Six Hours Away - Book Six
Charming Christmas - Book Seven

SWEET RIVER ~ THE SERIES
A Dream to Believe in - Book One
A Memory to Cherish - Book Two
A Song to Remember - Book Three
A Time to Forgive - Book Four
A Summer of Secrets - Book Five

A Moment in the Moonlight - Book Six

MOONBEAM BAY ~ THE SERIES
The Parker Women - Book One
The Parker Cafe - Book Two
A Heather Parker Original - Book Three
The Parker Family Secret - Book Four
Grace Parker's Peach Pie - Book Five
The Perks of Being a Parker - Book Six

INDIGO BAY ~ A multi-author sweet romance series

Sweet Days by the Bay - Kay's Complete Collection of stories in the Indigo Bay series

Or buy them separately:

Sweet Sunrise - Book Three
Sweet Holiday Memories - A short holiday story
Sweet Starlight - Book Nine

Sign up for my newsletter at my website *kaycorrell.com* to make sure you don't miss any new releases or sales.

CHAPTER 1

Evelyn Carlson hummed under her breath as she sat at her kitchen table and sorted through old recipes from her great-grandmother's collection. Many of the recipes had become favorites of the people who frequented the Sea Glass Cafe, and she didn't like to disappoint.

The peach pie—everyone called it *Grace's* peach pie after Grace Parker—was probably the favorite. Although, the cinnamon rolls were the second most requested item on the menu. Now she was browsing for something new to serve along with the patrons' favorites.

Here was one for a beef soup that sounded interesting. Maybe this winter. Right now, they were having an unseasonably warm late fall. She vaguely remembered a chilled strawberry soup that her grandmother used to make. Maybe she could find that recipe.

She got up and made herself a cup of tea and looked around her tiny but beloved apartment. She still couldn't believe she lived on her own for the first time in her life. She loved the absolute luxury of making her own decisions, decorating to her tastes, buying what she wanted for the place. Not that she'd spent much. Her daughter, Heather, had helped her find some furniture and decorations at the thrift shop. And she'd framed two lovely beach scenes Heather had painted and hung them on the wall. A glass bowl of seashells sat on the coffee table. Family pictures adorned a table near the sliding door to the balcony. The whole apartment was airy and coastal, and she adored it. Everything was perfect in her life right now. She couldn't remember ever being happier or more content.

She sat back down with her tea and the recipes and kept looking, hoping the right one would jump out at her and she could make something new. A card fell on the floor, and she leaned down to pick it up. She smiled when she saw it was the chilled strawberry soup recipe. She glanced over at the photo of Grace Parker sitting on the table across the room. "Thanks, Grace. I guess I'll try this one."

Rob Bentley stared at his phone screen and his sister's innocent yet not convincing, smile. "What did you just say?" He frowned, not truly believing he'd heard her correctly.

"I said I bought Murphy's Resort. You remember it from when we were kids, don't you? We'd go to Moonbeam for a week in the summer. I think we went like four times."

Oh, he remembered it all right. A tiny resort with ramshackle cabins. "Why would you buy it?" He couldn't wrap his mind around what his sister was saying. A resort? She bought a *resort?* And from what he could remember, the term *resort* was a generous name for the place. About eight or ten cottages. Loud, raucous window air-conditioning units that thumped into the night and never really cooled anything down. Pipes that knocked when the water ran and never enough hot water for showers. There had been a cracked windowpane in the cottage that had never been fixed over the years they'd gone there for vacation.

"It's what I wanted to do with my inheritance from Uncle Jeremy. It's all mine now, and I just love the town of Moonbeam."

He frowned again. "How long have you been there?"

"Um… just a few days." She shrugged "But I already know I'm going to love living here."

"Violet, those cottages were run down when we stayed there years ago."

Her infectious laugh came drifting across the airwaves. "Well, they aren't any better now. But with some paint and repairs, I'm sure this place will look great. Just wait and see."

He shook his head. "Why didn't you tell me you were considering this?"

She looked away from the screen before glancing back at it and grinning. "Because you'd have told me not to."

"I would have."

She waggled her finger. "Exactly my point."

"But you don't know anything about running a resort."

"I'll learn. And it's something that's all my own. Rob, I'm happy. Really happy. This is going to be great."

He seriously doubted it. It was probably yet another thing in a string of *great* things his sister was always getting into.

"So... the reason I'm calling is..." She gave him a wheedling smile, the one he'd rarely been able to resist in all of his baby sister's forty-something years. "I thought maybe you'd like to come to Moonbeam and... uh... help fix the place up. You love the beach. And you said you just finished your book. I know you always take a break when you finish a book."

He did need to take a break. She was right about that. Because he had absolutely no idea for his next book. None. Not one. At least not one that grabbed his attention enough to make him want to actually write it. "Just how much work does this place need?"

"Some." He didn't believe her innocent look this time, either. "But you're handy. You could do most of it."

He sighed. So his sister bought a place in Moonbeam and he'd get to spend his time off working on fixing the place. Though, maybe some mindless labor would help his writer's block.

"Come on, Rob, you know you want to come help. It will be fun. We can do it together."

He'd never so much as seen his sister pick up a single tool, so he wasn't so sure about the whole *together* thing.

"Please, Robby?"

Ah, the old Robby ploy. Unfortunately, it usually worked with him. And why had their uncle left her that money in the first place? He knew how Violet was prone to these harebrained ideas. Rob let out a long sigh. "Okay, I'll catch a plane out tomorrow. But I'm warning you, if the place is impossible, you're going to turn around and sell it. Even if you have to take a loss."

"It's not impossible. It's wonderful. Just you wait and see it. This is going to be great, you'll see. Thank you, Robby." A wide smile spread across her face as she clapped her hands. "By the time we're finished, it's going to be the best resort in Moonbeam."

He seriously doubted that. But he'd never been able to say no to her. "Okay, I'll see you tomorrow." Then he could see for himself what kind of mess she'd gotten herself into this time. Or, more accurately, gotten both of them into?

"And Robby? Don't look so worried." As usual, Violet got in the last word as she clicked off her phone. He was left staring at his screen saver.

CHAPTER 2

Evelyn went out into the cafe to help clear the tables after the lunch crowd. She'd been right about the chilled soup. It was a hit today. She'd have to put it in her recipe rotation.

The Jenkins twins stopped her as she walked past their table. "Evelyn, dear, the soup was fabulous. I'm not sure I've ever had a chilled soup before, but I know I adore everything you make, so I tried it. It was wonderful." One of the twins smiled at her.

She waited for a clue so she could figure out which one was which. You'd think by now she could tell them apart, but she still, after all these years, had no clue.

"I enjoyed it just as much as Jackie did." Jillian gave her the much-needed clue.

"I'm glad you both liked it. I'm sure I'll make it again soon."

"Oh, did you hear the news?"

What juicy town gossip did the twins have to share now? "I don't think so."

"Someone bought the old Murphy Resort. A woman. Looks to be in her forties? Can you imagine that? A young woman running the resort?" Jackie shook her head. "She sure has a lot of work to get that place back into shape. It's gotten so run down. I'm surprised Murphy could even find a buyer."

"I hope she's successful. It used to be a cute little place." Kind of. Murphy hadn't put a lot of energy into keeping it maintained. But she could see the potential in it. Possibly.

"I heard that Murphy moved to Sarasota after he sold the place." Jillian seemed eager to impart yet more of their town gossip.

Murphy was quite the character. Grumpy and standoffish. And the whole town just called him Murphy. She wasn't even sure what his first name was.

"Moonbeam is getting to be quite the town of woman-owned businesses. The Parker General Store. The Parker Cafe." Jillian listed them off on her fingers.

"And Margaret owns Barbara's Boutique," Evelyn added, not bothering to remind her—yet again—that it was actually Sea Glass Cafe. "That's another woman-owned business."

"That's right." Jackie turned to Jillian. "Maybe we should think of some kind of business to run."

"Maybe we should." Jillian frowned. "But what could we do?"

The twins had inherited a small family fortune. She'd never known them to have a job and couldn't quite imagine them going to work every day either.

"We should think about it." Jackie's face creased into a pensive look.

"We should," Jillian agreed.

"Well, I need to get back to work," Evelyn said. "Enjoy your afternoon." She gathered a tray of dishes and headed back into the kitchen.

Melody was busy rinsing dishes and putting them in the dishwasher. "Here, give me those. Should just about finish up this load." Melody reached for the tray.

"The Jenkins twins told me Murphy's Resort sold. Did you know that?"

"No, I didn't. I'm surprised Mr. Murphy found a buyer. The place is a mess."

"Well, he did. Some woman. She sure will have her work cut out for her." Evelyn turned to check on the dough she had rising for another batch of sourdough bread. Maybe the new owner would come into the cafe soon and she'd get a chance to meet her. Or maybe she'd bake something and drop by the cottages and introduce herself. Make the new owner feel welcome. Yes, that's what she should do.

Rob pulled his rental car into the drive to Murphy's Resort. Although *drive* was not quite what he'd call the grass-filled ruts that led to the main office, jarring his teeth as he drove over them. He climbed out of his car and looked around in disbelief. When they used to come here, the cottages had been painted a cheerful, if faded, color. Now it was hard to tell what color they actually had been. The door to one cottage was gaping open. Another cottage had a blue tarp covering its roof.

Had Violet even looked at this place before she bought it? He heard noise coming from the direction of the far cottage and headed that direction. He paused when he got to the beachside of the property and looked out over the white sand beach sprawling before him.

Now, *this* looked the same. The beach had always been his favorite part of staying here. That and the ice cream at the general store in town. He could only hope the store still existed and the ice cream was still as good. He stared at the waves rolling to shore and a pair of gulls swooping by. Royal palm trees lined the edge of the beach, providing a bit of shade without impeding the view. He regretfully pulled himself from the view and went to find Violet.

He walked over to where the noise was coming from and saw Violet standing with a man who was—his eyes widened in surprise— the man was putting in a central air conditioning unit.

Violet looked up, saw him, and grinned as she raced across the sand and threw herself into his arms. "Isn't it great?"

She finally released him, and he cocked his head to one side. "Great is not the word I would use to describe this." He swung his gaze around at the broken-down, neglected smattering of cottages. Sagging decking, broken windows, and the blue-tarped roof mocked him.

"It *will* be great. You'll see. Don't be so negative."

"And that guy?" He nodded toward the repairman.

"Oh, I set up that right after I bought the place. Putting in central air for each cottage."

"Putting in? You mean they still hadn't done that in all these years?"

"Nope."

"That must be costing you a pretty penny."

She shrugged. "It was in my budget. I knew I'd want to do this going into the purchase."

"You had a budget?"

She laughed. "Kind of. A rough idea. But things are costing more than I thought. But that's okay. I still have a little bit of the money left for the repairs."

"How little?"

"Some," she answered vaguely.

He let out a long sigh. "Okay, show me around the place so I know what I'm getting into here."

"Sure, come on." She grabbed his hand and tugged him toward the nearest cottage—which might possibly have been pink, but he sure couldn't tell from the minimal paint clinging to it…

She showed him each cottage, and each one needed a little more work than the one before. "And here is the work shed. Mr. Murphy left a lot of his tools, see?" She tugged on the door of the shed to open it. Or tried to. It was stuck. She kicked at the bottom, tugged again, and it opened. "See? Success." She waved her arm triumphantly.

He peered inside, glad to see some basics like a circular saw, drill, and a selection of random hammers and screwdrivers. If the saw and drill even worked...

He turned to Violet. "Are you sure this is what you want to do? It's going to take a lot of work."

"I'm positive."

Resigned, he pulled the door closed behind them. "Okay, let me get my stuff out of the car. I'll change and make a list of supplies we might need to get started."

"Perfect. I made up the guest room in the owner's cottage. It's attached to the back of the office."

"I don't suppose that cottage has central air..."

"Are you crazy? It was the first one I did. I'm

not living with a clunking window unit that doesn't cool the place down."

Okay, so his sister had made *one* decision that he totally agreed with.

CHAPTER 3

By late afternoon, Rob had put together a list of supplies he needed. A very long list. He headed into town and was pleased to see the general store was still in existence. He'd get his supplies and reward himself with ice cream—if they still had it.

Pushing through the door, he entered the store, surprised to see how much it had changed. More organized. Better lighting. Still quaint. But to his chagrin, no ice cream counter adorned the wall where it used to be.

A lady walked up to him and smiled. "Hi, can I help you?"

"Yes, I have a long list of supplies." He nodded toward the far wall. "But I'm disappointed the ice cream counter is gone."

She laughed. "Oh, it's not gone. We expanded to the building next door. It's over there along with a cafe."

His attitude brightened. Brightened a lot. He'd get his supplies, then treat himself. "So, I have this long list…"

"Let me look at it." The woman reached for it. "I'm Donna, by the way. My family owns the store."

He looked at her closely. "You wouldn't be one of the sisters who used to work at the ice cream counter when I'd come here in the summers, would you? Years and years ago."

"Guilty. We sure did."

"I came here to Moonbeam with my family for three or four summers."

"So you're back here and fixing something up?" Donna nodded at the list.

"Oh, that." He couldn't help himself. He rolled his eyes. "My sister bought a resort here and it… Let's just say it needs some work."

"The old Murphy place? I heard it had been sold."

"That very one." He shook his head. "I barely know where to start on it. But I've come for a visit to help her with repairs."

"By the looks of your list, there's a lot to do. Let's see what all we can find."

He followed after her and they found almost everything he needed, and she ordered in the items she didn't have. "Thanks for the help."

"Sure thing." She turned to a teenaged boy stocking shelves. "Blake, you want to load up these supplies for—" She turned back to him. "I didn't catch your name."

"Rob Bentley."

"If you don't mind giving Blake your keys, he'll load these into your trunk. And I'll take you next door to the cafe and you can have your ice cream. On the house."

"That sounds great." He tossed the keys to the boy. "Silver Ford, rental plates, right outside the door."

He followed Donna through an opening between buildings and entered the cafe, pleased to see the very same ice cream counter across the room. A few teenagers hung out at a table near the counter.

She nodded toward the table. "The kids come in for ice cream after school."

"Hi, Grams." A red-headed girl waved, and Donna waved back.

"My granddaughter and her friends." She

led him over to the counter. "Evelyn, this is Rob Bentley. He's wanting some ice cream. His sister is the one who bought the Murphy Resort, and he came to help her out."

He sat on a stool at the counter. "Hi, Evelyn. Nice to meet you. Though, I met you and your sister years ago."

"You did?" She looked at him expectantly.

"Came here years ago for vacation with my folks and my sister. You two worked the ice cream counter then. And to be honest, I've never had better ice cream anywhere."

"Secret family recipe." She smiled back at him.

"I'll leave you in Evelyn's capable hands. Oh, and Evie, I told him it was on the house."

Evelyn nodded. "So, Rob. What will you have?"

"If I remember correctly, all your flavors were good, but your vanilla was exceptional."

"Still is." She grinned. "Cone or bowl?"

"Cone, two scoops?"

"Coming up." She made his cone and handed it to him.

He tried it. Cold, creamy, with just the right amount of sweetness. Seriously, the best ice cream ever. "Just like I remembered. Maybe better."

"Not to brag, but I think we have the best ice cream in the world." Her sparkling eyes held a hint of laughter, but he could see she was proud of it.

"You won't hear me arguing with you."

Blake returned his keys and went over to the table with the teens. Evelyn tidied up the counter and chatted with him as he ate his cone. "So, your sister. She bought the Murphy Resort?"

"She did. Some wild idea because we stayed there a few times when we were young. I was a teen, she was a kid." He sighed. "But it needs a lot of work. A whole lot."

"I bet if they were fixed up they'd be wonderful. A great location and view. The beach is wonderful there. One of the best shelling areas around."

"Violet—that's my sister—has big plans for it. Thinks it will be wonderful."

"Violet. That's a pretty name. You don't hear it often anymore, but I love it."

"It was my grandmother's name. Vi's named after her."

"That's nice." Evelyn scrubbed the counter,

looked at it with a critical eye, then wiped some more.

"Violet's busy with repairs. She's already got a guy out there putting in central air in the cottages."

"That will help. It gets pretty hot and humid here in the summer."

"I remember. Those cottages were brutal during the day, and not much better at night. I slept out in a hammock they had near the beach quite a few of those nights." The ice cream was so good, he debated asking for another cone. Nah, that would be wrong, right?

"Good air conditioning will make them much more marketable," Evelyn agreed with Violet's decision, unaware of his ice cream dilemma.

"And the roofs fixed. And paint. Lots of paint. Both inside and outside."

Some customers came in and she held up a finger. "Be right back. Just let me wait on these men."

She chatted with two men, took their orders, and made malts for them. Her long, thick brown hair was pulled back in a practical braid. Her blue eyes sparkled as she laughed with the men.

They headed to a table with their malts and

she came back to him. "So how long are you staying?" she asked as she began to roll some silverware in napkins.

She never stopped. She cleaned, tidied, got orders, and now, made napkin rolls. All the while, chatting with customers. "I'm not sure. Maybe a month or so? I'm an author and I just finished a book and needed a break. Although this wasn't exactly what I had planned." He shrugged. "But I never can say no to Violet."

"What do you write?" She paused in her chores.

"Thrillers."

"Under Rob Bentley?"

"Robert Bentley." He didn't see any flicker of name recognition in her eyes, which told him she hadn't read his books, even if he considered himself a fairly successful author. Ah, well. It was always a reality check when someone hadn't heard of him.

He got up from the stool. "Thanks for the ice cream. I'm sure I'll be back in soon."

"Oh, wait there just a minute." Evelyn disappeared and came back with a package wrapped in a brown bag. "Here, I made this for Violet after I heard someone had bought the resort. I was going to drop it by and introduce myself. Will you give it to her?"

"Sure will."

"And bring her in. We'd love to get to know her."

"I'll do that." He nodded and headed toward the door, his mind already on his overwhelming to-do list as he left Sea Glass Cafe.

CHAPTER 4

Olivia hurried into Sea Glass Cafe to help with the dinner rush. With any luck, she'd get out before too late and have time to run by and see Austin. Their schedules hadn't been meshing very well recently, and she'd give anything to spend a couple quiet hours with him. They did have a date set up for tomorrow, but she'd love to see him tonight, too.

Evelyn looked up from where she was setting some pies to cool. "Hey, Livy."

"Hi." Olivia reached for a server apron, tied it on, and headed over toward her aunt. "Ethan is out there for dinner again," she whispered, making sure that Melody couldn't hear her.

"That's like three nights this week." Evelyn

grinned and turned toward Melody. "Mel, could you go see if anyone needs a refill on tea?"

"Of course." Melody dried her hands on a towel and headed out into the cafe.

"Oh, that was smooth," Olivia laughed. "Sending her out there knowing Ethan always orders a big glass of sweet tea."

"I'm doing what I can. I swear, Melody just cannot see that he's interested in her."

"And poor Ethan. He's so shy. I'm not sure when or if he'll get up the nerve to ask her out." She grabbed an order pad and slipped it into the pocket of the apron. "Okay, I'm off to work. Looks like we're really filling up this evening."

She worked steadily for hours, taking orders, bringing out meals, clearing tables, and chatting with customers. The time sped by, and she glanced at the clock and frowned. Later than she had hoped. When she heard the door open again, it took everything she had to keep from groaning at the last-minute customer as she turned around.

Instead she saw Austin, and she smiled in delight as she hurried over to him. "I was hoping I'd get to see you tonight." She gave him a quick kiss.

"I just have a couple of minutes.

Something's come up." Worry clouded his eyes. "My sister called, and Mom isn't doing well. I booked a late flight out. I'm already packed and my suitcase is in the car. Wanted to see you to say goodbye, though."

"Oh, Austin, I'm sorry about your mother." She wrapped her arms around him and held him for a moment.

"I am, too. She was doing better. This relapse—" He sighed. "Well, I want to get up there ASAP."

She let go of him and kissed his cheek. "Go, then. Call me when you get in, okay?"

"I will. I'm not sure how long I'll be gone."

"Don't worry about it. I'll still be here." She gave him an encouraging smile.

He nodded and kissed her quickly. "Got to run. I'll call."

And with that, he slipped outside. Her heart ached for what he was going through. Watching his mother suffer and fight her cancer. The roller coaster of remission and relapse. She wished she could do more to help him. But no matter how much she'd like to ease his burden, there wasn't a lot she could do except be here for him.

She turned and headed back to the kitchen,

her heart heavy and her mood somber. Evelyn looked up from where she was putting leftover muffins away in the fridge. "What's wrong?"

She plopped down in a chair. "It's Austin's mother. She's taken a turn for the worse. He left to go fly up and see her."

"Oh, that's too bad." Evelyn came over and rested her hand on her shoulder.

"I wish I could do something."

"I know you do. It's a hard time for him, I'm sure." Evelyn squeezed her shoulder. "Why don't you run along home? I'll finish up here."

"Are you sure?"

"Yes, go. And the walk home will do you good. Nothing like a nice evening walk to raise your spirits."

She slowly rose and nodded. "Okay, I think I'll take you up on your offer." She hung up her apron and headed out. The soft breeze and fresh, salty scent of the air helped, just like Evelyn had promised it would.

She was in no particular hurry and took the long way along the harbor, enjoying the familiar sights of her town. A few boats moored in the harbor bobbed in the moonlight. Someone was staying out on one of the boats. She could tell because faint lights shone through the cabin windows. Must be peaceful to sleep out there on a boat in the harbor. That's something she'd never done in all her years here.

The Jenkins twins were sitting outside on their porch. She waved to them as she passed by, and they called out a greeting. As she neared her home, she was pleased to realize she was feeling a bit better.

The house was all lit up when she arrived. Her daughter must be home. Music greeted her when she walked inside.

Emily looked up from where she perched on a stool by the kitchen counter with Blake beside her. "Hey, Mom. We're doing homework."

They had schoolbooks scattered in front of them and looked like they'd been hard at their assignments. Both were great students and took their studies seriously.

"Hi, Livy," Blake said. "Was it busy at the cafe tonight?"

"Surprisingly so."

She was glad that Emily and Blake had become such great friends. It couldn't have been easy for Blake to look for his birth parents—her cousin Heather and her boyfriend, Jesse—and move to Moonbeam after the death of the only mother he'd ever known. She liked to think her daughter had made the transition easier for him. And now Emily had a second cousin and couldn't be more pleased.

"You could have called me to come in if you needed help," he offered.

"We handled it, but thank you."

"I'm on the schedule for tomorrow evening."

"I am, too," Emily said. "Because tomorrow is your date night with Austin."

"Ah, he got called out of town." She wasn't really up to explaining it all again.

"That's too bad. Well, you can have the house to yourself and a night off. It will do you good."

That actually didn't sound all bad. A night alone. Maybe a long hot bath and a book. Or sitting out on the lanai and doing... nothing.

She made herself some ice water and turned to the kids. "I'm headed to bed to read for a bit. Lock the house and turn out the lights when Blake leaves, okay?"

"Sure. Night, Mom."

She headed to her room to escape into the

book she was reading. A new book by a new-to-her author, Robert Bentley. She hoped it didn't keep her up half the night reading like it had last night. It was *so* good.

CHAPTER 5

T he next morning Rob stood in the semi-grassy area in the middle of the circle of cottages. That sad excuse of a courtyard needed to be dealt with, too. Where to start?

If he could find a ladder, he could get up and see what was hiding beneath the blue tarp on that one roof. There was a window to be replaced in what he thought *might* be the green cottage.

Doing some exterior painting kind of appealed to him. But if he painted, he'd need another trip to town because Violet had given him a strict list of the colors she wanted for each cottage. Shades of teal, sunflower yellow, cotton-candy pink, mint green, sea green, and a coral color. Then a brighter shade of the same color for each door. He was fairly certain his idea of what these colors looked like would be different than Violet's.

Maybe he'd start on repairs, then head into town to get the paint.

Hours later Violet caught up with him in the probably green cottage as he was finishing up fixing a sagging board on the front porch.

"The repairman got another air conditioning unit hooked up. His vent guy is pretty quick at adding in the new air ducts." She looked at the front porch and nodded approvingly. "Hey, are you hungry? It's way past lunchtime."

"I'm starving." His stomach rumbled to add emphasis to his words.

"I could make us sandwiches," she offered. "We still have plenty of that sourdough loaf you brought home last night."

The parcel Evelyn asked him to pass along to his sister had turned out to be a loaf of homemade bread and strawberry jam. Sliced, toasted, and buttered, it had made a wonderful addition to breakfast this morning.

"How about we go into town and eat at Sea

Glass Cafe instead? Then I could pick up the paint, and you can make sure I get the right shades."

"That sounds perfect."

"Have you eaten there yet?" Violet helped him put his tools away in the shed.

"No, I've been too busy to do much of anything but work on the cottages."

"They have the same ice cream they had at the general store when we were kids." His mouth watering at the memory of yesterday's ice cream, he led Violet to the car.

"Really? I remember you loved it."

"What can I say? Ice cream is my Achilles heel. And I still do love it. Come on." They drove to the cafe, his stomach rumbling the whole time. He wondered if he could have ice cream for dessert *before* his lunch…

He held the door open for his sister and they went into the cafe. The aroma of fresh bake bread, a hint of cinnamon, and strong coffee assaulted his senses. His stomach growled in anticipation.

Evelyn called out a greeting to them as they entered. "Welcome back, Rob."

His sister glanced at him, a slight frown

creasing her brow. "How do you already know people here in town and how do they know your name?"

"I'm just a friendly kind of guy." He elbowed her as they walked over to Evelyn. "This is my sister, Violet. Vi, this is Evelyn."

"Nice to meet you."

"Oh, Evelyn. Thank you so much for the bread. It's wonderful. What a nice gift."

"I'm glad you liked it. Just a little something to welcome you to town," Evelyn said as she led them to a table. "So you bought the old Murphy Resort, I hear."

"I did." Violet laughed and poked him. "Much to Rob's chagrin. But it's going to be great when we finish fixing it up."

"And by we, she means me," Rob said as he took his seat. Violet sent him an exasperated glare, and he grinned back at her.

Evelyn handed them menus, then pointed to the chalkboard. "Special today is meatloaf sandwich or BLT. We also have a chicken salad. And the regular items on the menu."

"I'll have the meatloaf sandwich and tea." It sounded substantial, and he was famished.

"I'll have the chicken salad and tea." Violet

looked around the cafe. "This place is so adorable. And look at all the sea glass in the vases. And the decorations. I just love it. I want the cottages to have this same welcoming, homey feel."

"Thank you. We're pretty proud of the cafe. Haven't been open a year yet, but business is good." Evelyn beamed at the praise. She had the warmest smile. Very welcoming. And friendly eyes that sparkled when she spoke. "I'll go get your orders."

She headed to the kitchen. Today her hair was pulled up in a twisted knot thing on top of her head. Her cheeks were slightly flushed. Probably from the heat in the kitchen.

"You're staring." Violet nudged his foot under the table.

"I am not."

"Are so."

"Whatever." He rolled his eyes, but he knew full well he had been staring.

Evelyn returned with their tea. "Here you go. I'll have your meals out in a jiffy. Melody is getting them ready."

He took a sip of the tea. It was excellent, which didn't surprise him.

"You two should save room for dessert. Fresh peach pie."

"That I will. With a scoop of your delicious vanilla ice cream on top." He smiled at Evelyn, and she rewarded him with a smile of her own. It wouldn't take much to convince him to keep popping in here for meals.

Violet kicked him under the table, and he had to refrain from kicking her back. He was the *mature* sibling. His foot twitched under the table.

Evelyn went back to the kitchen, and he was disappointed that a new woman—Melody, she introduced herself—brought out their meals.

"I hope you enjoy your meals," Melody said. "Evelyn said you bought Murphy's place. I'm so glad someone is going to fix it up. It's on such a lovely spot of the beach. The view is wonderful there."

"See, Melody thinks I made a good decision to buy the place." Violet sent him a gloating smile.

"I'm not sure that's what she said exactly." Was he going to have to permanently roll his eyes at his sister?

As Melody left, they turned to their lunches. His was delicious with generous portions which he managed to finish. Soon, Evelyn came out with their peach pie. He took one bite and realized he'd reached the ultimate in foodie pleasure. The peaches were just sweet enough with a hint of cinnamon. The crust was flakey and perfectly browned. "This is honestly the best peach pie I've ever tasted."

"Thank you. It's Grace Parker's peach pie. My great-grandmother. Old family recipe."

"Like the ice cream?"

"Exactly." She nodded soberly, although her eyes crinkled as she hid a grin. "So, how are repairs going?"

"They're going great. Getting air-conditioning put in," Violet said. "And Rob here, when he's not busy complaining, is working on repairs to—I don't know—stuff."

"Right, I'm busy with stuff." He caught himself right before he rolled his eyes. "Windows, decking, roofing, plumbing. You name it, it needs to get done."

"And painting." Violet turned to Evelyn. "I'm going to paint each cottage a nice bright color. It's going to look great."

"I bet it will."

"See, she thinks buying the cottages was a

good idea, too. Just like Melody." Another gloating smile.

He had to admit his sister was enthusiastic about her purchase, even if he thought it was a foolish investment. There was something to be said for her being this happy. Hopefully, it stayed that way when she realized the hard work and long hours that went into running a resort. But she had always wanted something to call her own as she bopped from job to job. As much as he hated to admit it, maybe this was exactly what she needed.

"You two should come to the Sandcastle Festival this weekend. It's right down the beach from the resort. Near the big gazebo at the town beach. Do you know where that is?"

"I do," Violet said. "That sounds like fun."

"There are people who come from all around and make the most fantastic sandcastles. Very elaborate. And then there's a kids' competition and that's cute too. It's Saturday. And there'll be lots of food booths there. The cafe will have a booth."

"With ice cream?" He grinned.

"Yes, we'll have sandwiches and ice cream cones."

"I'll be there."

"Great. I'll see you both there. Thanks for coming in." She turned and headed back to the kitchen, and he deliberately looked away. But Violet wasn't having any of it. She grinned and shook her head.

"What?" He glared at her.

CHAPTER 6

E mily sat in the lunchroom at school with Blake and some of her friends. Blake and Angela Healey were deep in a discussion about a calculus problem that neither had solved. They were oblivious to the noise around them. The talking. Laughter. The clatter of trays.

She watched them thoughtfully. Angela was quiet, a bit of a nerd, with straight brown hair and big black glasses. She had a wry sense of humor and took school seriously. Which actually made her a perfect match for Blake.

She scowled when she saw Jeanie Francis heading their way. Would the girl never get the clue that Blake wasn't interested in her?

Jeanie plopped down in the chair across from him. "Hi, Blake."

He looked up, and she caught the slightly annoyed look before he hid it. "Uh, hi, Jeanie."

"Whatcha working on?"

"Angela is helping me with this calculus problem."

"At lunchtime? Lunch is when we get to take a break." Jeanie leaned over and closed the calculus book. "Want to go outside and get some fresh air?"

Blake carefully opened up the book and gave Angela an apologetic look before turning to Jeanie. "No, I really want to figure this out. If we do, there's extra credit."

"But I wanted to talk to you." Jeanie placed a careful pout on her face.

Emily bit her tongue so she wouldn't say something she shouldn't.

"I'm kinda busy right now. Can we talk later?"

Jeanie let out a long-suffering sigh. "I guess so. I still don't know why you're doing schoolwork during lunch break." She stood, tossing her curls as she shook her head before flouncing away.

"You can go with her if you want," Angela said as she looked down at the paper in front of her.

Blake shook his head. "Nah, let's get back to figuring out this problem. I really could use the extra credit."

Emily watched the two of them from the side of her eyes. She was pretty sure Angela was crushing on Blake. Blake seemed oblivious to it. Typical guy. To his credit, though, Angela was nowhere near as obvious as Jeanie Francis.

Emily, Angela, and Jeanie had all grown up together. In grade school, Angela and Jeanie were actually best friends, but by middle school, Jeanie had moved on to who she considered the cool kids and left Angela in the dust. Probably because Angela was a bit overweight back then. She'd gotten the big black glasses in middle school, dressed in baggy clothes to cover her weight, and kept to herself most of the time. She'd slimmed down over the past couple years, not that her outfits had changed.

Emily glanced over at Angela. Her clothes today were a bit loose and ill-fitting. Like she'd never gotten over being overweight and trying to hide it. She kept shoving her glasses back up in place. Emily bit her bottom lip. What she wouldn't give for a sixty-minute Cinderella makeover with Angela.

Angela was a pretty girl, but she never wore

makeup or clothes that might be better suited to her. It seemed like she liked to fade into the background and not be noticed. But there was this slight vibe that maybe Angela was tired of not being noticed, of being in the background.

She bit her lip, not knowing how the makeover could ever happen without it being awkward. It wasn't like she could say something like—um, hey, can I help you dress, do your hair, and maybe pick out some clothes that suit you better? Crazy thoughts.

She stood and grabbed her things. "Hey, Blake, I'll see you at work later."

He looked up quickly and nodded. "Okay, see you."

"Angela, you should stop by after school and get some ice cream. On the house for helping him with this calculus problem."

"Oh, thanks. Maybe I will." Angela gave her a tentative smile.

"You should." She walked away, glancing back once to see both of them sitting with their heads almost touching, poring over the math problem. She grinned as she headed off to her locker, hoping Angela would take her up on the offer.

Shortly after Emily and Blake started their shift, Emily looked up to see Angela come into the cafe. Perfect. She elbowed Blake as he cleared off a table. "I've got those. Go wait on Angela."

Blake looked up and she swore a faint blush crossed his cheeks. She smothered a grin. *Aha!* There was something there.

Blake headed over to the ice cream counter and made Angela a malt. Angela sat on the last stool, a bit away from another group of kids from their high school.

She finished clearing up the dishes for Blake and took them to the kitchen before heading back out to the ice cream counter. Another group of kids from the high school came in. "Hey, Blake, why don't you finish up with the napkin rolls and I'll get these orders."

He could roll napkins and chat with Angela, couldn't he? Besides, rolling silverware ranked right up there with filling salt and pepper shakers on her list of jobs she hated at the cafe. She'd much rather be waiting on customers and chatting with them. That part of the job was fun.

After about an hour, things slowed down and most of the customers drifted away. Angela got up to leave. "Thank you for the malt. It was really good."

"Come in anytime. It's a great place to hang out after school." Maybe she could encourage her to come by more often. Blake would like that, even if he wouldn't admit it.

Angela nodded and smiled. "Bye, Blake."

"Bye, Angela." The dopey look on his face as he watched Angela leave said it all.

She walked over and elbowed him. "So... you like her, don't you?"

"I don't know. I guess so." There was that blush again.

"So ask her to the Sandcastle Festival. You guys could walk around. See the sandcastles. Eat too much junk food."

"I don't know... I mean, we're just friends."

"Is that all you want it to be? Friends?"

"I wouldn't want to mess things up."

"I swear guys can be so clueless." She let out a long sigh. "I'm betting that she likes you."

"How do you know?" His eyebrows furrowed, and he looked toward the door as if she'd still be there.

"Trust me. I can tell."

"I don't know…"

"You're so impossible sometimes." She grabbed the tray of napkin rolls from in front of him. "You should ask her." She stalked away, wondering if he'd take her advice or not.

Evelyn and Donna walked through Parker's General Store and Sea Glass Cafe, checking on things, doing their nightly closing-up routine. When they were done, Evelyn met Donna at the front door, and they stepped outside into the fresh evening air.

Donna locked the door behind them and touched the plaque beside the door that said established in 1926.

"Just like grandmother and her mother did when they closed up for the day," Evelyn said.

"Some traditions are good to keep. It makes me feel more connected to the Parker women who went before us."

"It's a nice tradition." She wanted to touch it too but somehow felt like it was Donna's thing to do. That she'd be intruding on the tradition.

After all, Donna was the one who had taken over running the store for years. Donna and Livy had just recently asked her to be partners in the business with them. She eyed the plaque once more, then ignored it.

"Busy day at the store today." Donna stretched and looked up and down the street.

"Busy at the cafe, too. It's strange how sometimes a weekday will be almost as busy as a weekend day." Evelyn tilted her head from side to side, trying to release the tension in her shoulders. "But I'm not complaining, really."

Donna nodded. "I'm not either."

"So, that Rob guy came in today and brought his sister. The one who bought Murphy's Resort," Evelyn said as they headed down the sidewalk together.

"He came into the store today, too, so I got to meet Violet. They bought gallons and gallons of paint for the cottages."

"She said she was going to paint each one a different color."

"Well, I'll say this. Judging by the colors she picked, they are going to be *bright*. But she did a great job picking the tones. I think they'll all work really well together."

"I can't wait to see how it all turns out." Evelyn paused as they got to the corner where she split off from Donna and would head to her apartment. "I told them about the Sandcastle Festival, too. They both said they'd come."

"That reminds me. I told Emily and Blake they could work the morning shift at the booth that day but have the afternoon off. Kids gotta be kids sometimes, don't they?"

"They do. And both of them work really hard. An afternoon of fun will be good for them."

"You want to come over to my house for a bit?" Donna asked. "Barry is working late."

She considered it, but she really was tired from the long day of work. Plus, she loved going home to her cozy little apartment. "I think I'll just head home. I'm beat."

"Okay, I'll see you tomorrow."

Donna continued down the sidewalk and Evelyn turned toward her apartment. The streetlights switched on as she walked down the street as if welcoming her home.

As she slowly strolled along, she realized how content she was with her life these days. How pleased she was with the life she'd created.

She loved things just like they were. Predictable. Stable. Exactly how she liked things to be.

She slowed as she saw a man approaching and realized who it was. "Good evening, Rob," she said as he got closer.

"Well, Evelyn. Hello." Smile lines crinkled the edges of his eyes as he greeted her.

"Just out for an evening walk?" she asked, noticing how relaxed he looked.

"My sister had me painting samples of the paint colors on the different cottages and was second-guessing her choices. Anyway, I figured if I didn't insist I wanted a walk, she'd have me working until midnight." He shook his head, but she could tell that he wasn't really annoyed.

"Donna said she liked the colors Violet picked out."

"I hope she tells Violet that if she goes back for more paint. I think they look good, but I don't know coral from peach from orange, evidently. Oh, and teal can be blueish or greenish, or so I've been told. And it has to be the perfect teal shade." He shrugged.

"I'm sure she'll sort it out."

"She will." He glanced down the street. "I'm not headed anywhere in particular. Just out stretching my legs. Mind if I walk you home?"

She looked at him in surprise, not expecting that. "I... ah..."

"No, that's okay. I know you don't really know me or anything." He stepped back.

"No, I'd like the company. I'm just down this street and left on the next."

He fell into stride beside her. "Nice to live where it's pleasant weather for evening walks. Pretty chilly back home now. I live in Vermont."

"It is nice. Even summer nights are okay for me, though some people complain about the humidity. I think the gulf stirs the air enough, and we often have a good breeze." She smiled. "I love living here."

"It's a nice little town."

"It is. Has everything I need. And the people are friendly. My family is here. It's just... nice."

"Not to mention you have ice cream available whenever you want it." He grinned at her.

"There's that, too." A smile tugged at her lips as she recalled how he'd relished his peach pie with ice cream.

"I seriously remember how wonderful that ice cream was from back in my childhood. Made quite the impression."

She laughed. "I guess so. That was a long time ago."

They paused in front of her apartment building and stood under the streetlight. "Thanks for letting me join you on your walk home. Enjoyed the company." An easy smile played at the corners of his mouth.

"I enjoyed the company, too."

"I better head out or Violet will be sending out a search party."

"You know the way back to the resort from here?" Moonbeam wasn't a big town, but its streets wove this way and that and sometimes got confusing.

He nodded, gave her another smile, and headed back the way they had come. She watched him go until he faded into the distance.

Rob seemed like a nice guy. And it was kind of him to help his sister out with the resort. He had a nice quick smile, too. An easy smile. And his warm brown eyes twinkled when he teased his sister. And even with his protests, she could tell he adored her.

A couple came out of the building and said hi, and she decided she couldn't just stand there all night thinking about the newcomer to town, now could she? She slipped past them and into the lobby.

She couldn't wait to get up to her apartment, make a cup of tea, and curl up with a good book. A perfect end to the day as far as she was concerned.

CHAPTER 7

Heather had taken to dropping by Jesse's a couple mornings a week to have coffee with him. Or so that was her excuse. She really loved seeing Blake off to school.

Blake came into the kitchen where she and Jesse were sipping coffee. He dropped his school bag on the floor. "Hey, Heather."

"Morning." She took in every detail. His damp hair from his shower, the sleep that still clung to his face as if trying to lure him back to bed.

"Can I make you breakfast?" Jesse rose.

"Nah, I'm just going to grab a granola bar. I'm heading to school early to meet someone to work on some stuff."

"That would be Angela?" Heather asked.

He stared at her. "Yes... but..." Then he laughed. "Emily talked to you, huh?"

"She might have mentioned something."

He sunk down on a chair across from her. "Emily says Angela likes me. She says she can tell."

"Do you like her?"

"Maybe. Yeah, I... I do." He nodded.

"You going to ask her out?" Heather looked over the top of her coffee cup, studying his face carefully.

"I don't know. I haven't really dated before. First, Mom was sick. Then when I moved to my aunt's, I didn't have much luck making friends there."

"So, you're saying this would be your first date ever?" Heather stored away this detail she did not know about her son.

Blake nodded sullenly. "Yeah. That's lame, right?"

"No, it's not lame," Jesse chimed in. "But you should ask her out if you want to. What's the worst that can happen?"

"She'll say no? She'll laugh at me? I ruin us just being friends?" Blake scowled.

"Sometimes you have to take chances to get what you want." Heather offered the advice and for a moment felt very motherly, a feeling that suited her just fine.

"Maybe. We'll see." Blake rose. "I gotta run. See you tonight, Jesse."

"I'm on The Destiny until we dock. You want to wait for a late dinner?"

"Nah, I'll grab something at the cafe or something."

"Okay, have a good day." Jesse frowned at the empty space where Blake had been.

"What's wrong?" she asked.

Jesse sighed. "I feel like I'm always trying to balance everything. Being a father to Blake. Running The Destiny. And I feel like I'm falling short in both areas."

"I'm pretty sure that every working parent feels that way." She reached over and took his hand. "And you should let me help more. I can make Blake dinner when you're busy. Or anything else that would help." Truth be told, she was so jealous that Jesse got to live with Blake every single day.

"I'll sort it out." Jesse rose and took his cup to the sink.

She got up, put her cup in the sink along with his, and stood beside him. "The offer still stands. I'd love to see more of Blake."

He turned and pulled her into his arms. "I know. And I want you to have more time with him. It's just that everything still feels so new and I'm trying to find my way with him."

"And you don't want to throw me into the mix?" That thought hurt her feelings, but she understood where he was coming from.

He sighed. "It's not that. It's just that we're still trying to figure things out between us—you and me. Add that to trying to figure things out with Blake. Figuring out the whole father thing. It's a lot."

She stepped back and looked directly at him. "And I'd like the opportunity to figure out the *mother* thing, too," she whispered.

Jesse's eyes widened, and after a moment, he nodded. "You're right. I know you do."

And yet, he didn't ask for help. Didn't offer her more time with Blake. "I—I should go." She turned and walked out of the cottage.

Jesse Brown could sometimes be the most infuriating, clueless man. He should let her help more. She *wanted* to help. But he seemed to think he was going to figure out some kind of magic playbook all on his own for dealing with all of this.

And she was pretty certain that eventually

he would find out it wasn't going to work like that…

Emily sat with Blake and Angela at lunch again. Today they weren't trying to decode calculus. They were celebrating that they'd conquered yesterday's problem and both been given extra credit.

"You two math geeks did pretty well figuring that problem out. I heard no one else in the class did." Emily took a sip of her drink.

"We did. We rocked it. I couldn't have figured it out without Angela's help." Blake smiled at Angela.

Angela blushed.

Emily grinned.

That was until she saw Jeanie Francis heading their way. "Incoming." She nodded her head toward Jeanie and was rewarded with a frown from Blake.

Jeanie slid into the chair beside her. "There you are, Blake. I was looking for you. I've decided you should take me to the Sandcastle Festival."

"I... uh..." Blake sent a wild look toward Emily.

She raised an eyebrow and let him find his way out of this one. He was going to have to get tough with Jeanie. Spell it out for her that he wasn't interested.

"Everyone is going to be there. We'll have fun. You can pick me up about eleven. I don't want to miss the sandcastle competition. Well, the adult one. I don't care about the kids' one."

Of course she didn't. She probably didn't even like kids. Emily thought the kids' competition was adorable.

"No, I... uh... I already have plans."

Jeanie's eyes narrowed. "Don't tell me you're going with your *cousin*." She said the word cousin like it was a forbidden, dirty word.

Emily sat back and waited to see what Blake would say. He looked at Jeanie, then at Angela. "No, I was hoping to take Angela to the festival," he blurted out.

Angela's eyes widened. "You were?"

"You are? You want to take *her*?" Jeanie scowled.

Blake turned to Angela. "Will you go with me to the festival?

Angela blushed a deep red and her eyes widened. "Yes," she replied softly.

"But—" Jeanie glared at all of them. "You can't mean you want to take *her* instead of me?"

"Yes, I do," Blake said firmly.

Jeanie jumped up, her chair crashing to the floor behind her. She leaned close to Angela. "He's out of your league."

Angela's mouth dropped open.

"Hey." Blake stood. "Cut it out, Jeanie."

"I can't believe you'd turn me down to go with her." Jeanie's eyes flashed in fury.

Emily looked at Jeanie. "Don't you have somewhere to go?"

"I do. And it's way far away from all of you losers." She flounced away, curls bobbing in anger, her shoulders set.

"I guess she's finally figured out you're not interested in her." She looked over at Angela, who sat there in shock. "You okay? Jeanie can be pretty mean when she wants to."

"I… uh… I'm fine." She turned to Blake. "Do you really want to take me to the festival, or was that just a way to turn down Jeanie?"

"No, I really want to take you. I've been trying to get my nerve up to ask you." He gave her a wry grin. "This wasn't exactly how I expected to do it, but I guess it worked."

Angela nodded. "It worked. I'd like to go with you."

"Okay, that's settled, and now hopefully Jeanie got the hint and will leave us alone." Emily looked across the table at the two of them staring at each other with goofy smiles on their faces. Ah, young love. She hid her grin and sipped her drink, glad that Blake had finally set Jeanie straight.

Blake finally stood. "I've got to go turn in a paper to Miss Brady. I'll see you after school?" He looked at Angela.

"Sure."

"Maybe we could walk over and get ice cream at Parker's."

"I'd like that."

"Okay, cool." Blake hurried away.

After he left, Angela turned to her, panic in her eyes. "You have to help me."

"Sure. What do you need?"

Angela blushed again. "I've got nothing to wear. Not on a date. You always look so put together without it being over the top, you know?"

"I just know what I like. But I could take you

shopping. Tomorrow after school? I'm not working then." Emily relished the idea of shopping with Angela. This was going to be great.

"That would be wonderful. And… maybe we could pick out some new school clothes for me, too?"

"Of course." It was getting better and better. "I'll meet you at Barbara's Boutique tomorrow after school."

Angela stood. "Thank you, Emily. You're a lifesaver."

Emily watched her cross the lunchroom and smiled to herself. Things were working out better than she'd hoped. Blake had asked out Angela. Jeanie was hopefully going to leave them alone, and Angela had asked her to take her shopping. Productive lunch hour.

CHAPTER 8

R ob looked at his handiwork on the roof. The repair hadn't been as involved as he'd thought. And now, as his reward, there was no more blue tarp. He climbed down the ladder and went in search of Violet, who, to his surprise, was painting the teal cottage.

"Whoa, look at you." He grinned as he walked up to her.

"Hey, I know how to paint." She stood back and frowned. "But it looks kind of streaky."

"Let it dry and give it another coat."

"Okay. I hope this turns out the right shade. I have it all in my mind how I want the cottages to look."

"I'm sure it will be fine." Looked fine to

him, even if he wasn't sure if this was her teal or her seafoam green cottage.

"I'm going to paint all the cottages and leave you with the other repairs." She stood with her hand on her hip and her lips set in a firm line of determination.

"That's a lot of work." He struggled to hide his doubt.

"It's something I can do. I don't know how to do the wood repairs, or plumbing, or roof repairs. This I can do."

He swallowed his lingering skepticism and said, "Hey, I'm going to head into town. Need a few supplies. Do you need anything?"

"Nah, I'm good. I'm determined to finish this side of the cottage."

He might stop by Sea Glass Cafe, too. And he even tried to pretend it was the ice cream calling him, not the hope that he'd run into Evelyn. He drove into town and popped into the cafe. Pleasure swept through him when he saw Evelyn behind the ice cream counter. "Good afternoon," he said as he approached.

She rewarded him with a welcoming smile. "Ah, your daily ice cream fix, I see."

"It has sort of become a routine for me,

hasn't it?" He slipped onto a barstool. "I'm actually craving a piece of your peach pie, too."

"You're in luck. I have about half a pie left. I'll get you a slice." Her eyes twinkled. "And I bet you want that scoop of vanilla on top."

"You've already figured me out. My weakness for your peach pie and ice cream."

She disappeared to the kitchen and returned with a slice of pie, which she mounded a huge scoop of vanilla ice cream onto before placing it in front of him.

He took a bite and couldn't decide which was better. The pie or the ice cream. He was going to have to start exercising if he kept up with this new diet. "It's really delicious."

"Thank you." She paused in her work and leaned against the counter across from him. "Repairs coming along okay on the resort?"

"Slowly. Not sure when she'll be able to open." He shook his head. "And she's insisting that she's going to paint each cottage herself while I work on other repairs. That's going to take her forever. But there is no changing Violet's mind when she has it set on something." He had a grudging admiration for her determination, though.

"I'm sure when it's done, she'll be proud of all her hard work."

"I still haven't looked at her reservation system or much about the business side. We're going to sit down tonight and go over some of that. I'm beginning to wonder when I'm ever going to make it back home." He shrugged. "Although, I could be talked into spending more time here. Vermont winters can be brutal."

"If you need any techie help, Austin Woods —he's engaged to my niece, Livy—he's really good with that kind of thing. He does websites and social media. He helped get the cafe's online ordering system going."

"I'll keep that in mind."

Evelyn pushed away from the counter. "I know someone for everything here in Moonbeam. If you need a plumber or an electrician, let me know. I have the name of a general handyman, too. Two, actually. The Keating brothers. They're retired but work at Parker's on Sunday. They also do odd jobs around town."

"I guess you know just about everyone in town."

She laughed. "Pretty much."

He looked over his shoulder when she waved

to someone. Two identical women were entering the cafe.

"Oh, Evelyn, dear. We were walking by and I told Jackie that we must come in and get some ice cream. Aren't we wicked? Sweets in the middle of the day." The twins walked up to the counter and looked at him.

"Jackie, Jillian, this is Rob. His sister bought Murphy's Resort, and he's in town helping her."

"Oh, so good to meet you," Jillian said and reached out and pumped his hand. "We're thrilled the old resort is getting all spruced up. It was getting to be such an eyesore. Murphy just let the place go. Didn't keep up with repairs. And it's needed paint on those cottages forever."

"Pleased to meet both of you. And my sister is working on the paint. Hope you like bright colors."

"Oh, that will look so cheerful." Jackie gave him a wide, approving smile. "What made your sister decide to buy the resort? Is she in the hospitality business?"

He laughed. "Not exactly. At least not before buying this resort. We did stay there a few times when we were kids."

"Ah, fond memories, I bet," Jillian said.

He nodded. Not particularly fond memories

of the resort itself. The place had been run down even back then. But he *did* have fond memories of the ice cream at Parker's.

"Well, we wish her all the best." Jackie turned to Evelyn. "I'll have a scoop of vanilla in a bowl. And some sprinkles on top. I do like sprinkles."

"I think I'll have the same," her twin said.

"You two take whatever table you want and I'll bring it over to you."

"It was nice to meet you. We hope to meet your sister soon." The twins headed over to a table by the window.

"Just to let you know, anything you say to the twins can and will be broadcast to the town," Evelyn whispered, leaning close. "They have good hearts, but they do like to know what's going on in everyone's lives... and don't mind letting other people know, too."

"Okay, I'm forewarned." They seemed like rather harmless, personable ladies to him, but what did he know about small-town gossip?

Melody came out of the kitchen. "Evelyn, let me take over here. It looks like your bread dough is ready to be made into loaves and I know you wanted to try out that fancy braid with this batch."

"Okay, thank you. The twins ordered vanilla scoops in bowls with sprinkles."

"I'm on it."

"I'll see you soon," Evelyn said, and then, much to his disappointment, turned and disappeared into the kitchen

"Hi, Rob. Having a nice day?" Melody asked with a friendly smile.

He nodded and gave her an automatic smile in reply. Melody was a nice, friendly woman, but he much preferred Evelyn working the counter. He'd probably have to come back tomorrow for more ice cream…

CHAPTER 9

"Hey, Aunt Evelyn." Livy hurried into the kitchen and grabbed an apron. "Melody just introduced me to that Rob Bentley I keep hearing about. Did you know that he's *Robert* Bentley, the author? I just finished one of his books. It was so good."

"You know his writing?"

"Yes, a thriller writer. So good. Great characters. Does a good job with the locations. And the plot twists. Wow."

"Hm." She'd have to pick up one of his books and try it.

"He seems like a nice guy."

Evelyn nodded. He did seem like a nice guy. And certainly a good brother. "Yes, he's nice," she said noncommittally. After all, he was just one of many customers at the cafe.

"And guess who just came in? Ethan Chambers. I told Melody to take his order." Livy grinned. "I swear, that woman is never going to get the hint."

"Maybe she's not ready to date anyone. She's only been a widow for a year or so. That was a big adjustment for her."

And maybe she was talking more about herself than Melody. Living alone was a big adjustment after years of being a couple. Of being a wife. But she liked her life now. And Melody, for that matter, seemed happier these days after starting work at Parker's.

"The kids just came in for ice cream too. Emily, Blake, and Angela. You know Angela, Charlene Healey's daughter? Emily pulled me aside and said that Blake has a date with Angela for the festival this weekend."

Her grandson had a date? That was news. "Does Heather know?"

"I'm not sure, but I'm meeting her at Jimmy's tonight after the cafe closes. I'll ask her then."

"I haven't seen her in days. She must be busy working on those illustrations for that children's book. I admit, I kind of liked it when she helped us out when we were first opening the cafe. I got to see her every day."

"You could come to Jimmy's tonight with us," Livy offered.

"No, you two go have your cousin time. I'll catch up with her soon. If nothing else, I'm sure I'll see her at the festival."

"You will. She's got some of her illustrations at the art booth. She's donating the proceeds to the children's home program that Ted's niece runs. Heather and Cassandra chatted about it the last time Cassandra was in town. Heather was really impressed with the work Cassandra is doing. So, she decided to put some of her artwork up and donate the proceeds."

"That's nice of her." But it didn't surprise her. Her daughter had a very kind heart.

"Heather loves a good cause. And I think after Blake came so close to being put in a foster home that it hits kind of close for her." Livy walked over and peeked out the kitchen door. "Melody is still standing there chatting with Ethan. That's a good sign, right?"

She shrugged. "I don't know. Ethan is going to have to get a bit more deliberate if he wants Melody to take notice."

"So, what can I help you with here in the kitchen while I hide out and let Melody chat with Ethan?"

"I could use some help with the oatmeal cookies. Just need to use the scoop and drop them on those two cookie sheets."

"Perfect. I'll get started."

Heather sat at the bar at Jimmy's nursing a beer, waiting for Livy. She knew Livy would make it whenever things got wrapped up at the cafe. Some nights it was later than others. She didn't mind waiting though. It was a lovely night. Cool breeze. One of her favorite guitar players, Dave Post, was playing ballads at the far end of the deck overlooking the harbor. The music drifted over to her. Some sad ballad about shipwrecks and storms.

"Sorry I'm late." Livy hopped on the barstool beside her and motioned to the bartender to get her a beer. "And I have news."

She looked at her cousin expectantly. The perk of working in the cafe was she often found out town news quickly. "Town gossip?"

"Nope. News about Blake."

"Tell me." Heather waited impatiently as Livy reached for the beer the bartender handed her and took a sip.

"He has a date. This weekend. For the festival."

A smile crept across her face. He'd done it. Asked out Angela. He must have taken her motherly advice. "That's good news. Angela Healey, right?"

"How did you know?"

"He was talking about her this morning at breakfast. Said he was interested in her. I told him to take a chance and ask her out."

"He must have taken your advice. And Emily said she's going shopping with Angela tomorrow after school. Angela wants Emily to help her pick out some new clothes. I think she's a really cute girl. Smart, too, according to Emily. Emily likes her a lot."

"If Emily likes her, I do, too. Emily is a great judge of character."

Livy beamed at the praise of her daughter. "I think so."

"You're a great Mom, Liv. You really are."

"And it looks like you're getting the hang of this mom thing, too." Livy raised her beer bottle. "To motherhood—even with all its challenges."

"Motherhood." Heather clinked her bottle with Livy's. It was strange to think of herself as a mother. Although technically, she had been since the day Blake was born. But still, the opportunity to be in his life now? It still amazed her that she'd been given this chance.

"So, you're going over to Jesse's for breakfast now?" Livy raised an eyebrow. "Is this a daily thing?"

"No, not *daily*." Okay, she had gone three times this week, but who's counting?

"How's Jesse doing these days?" Livy set her bottle on the bar.

"He's... exasperating. He's so overwhelmed with everything. The Destiny, Blake, the legal stuff."

"Trying to balance running a company and being a parent is hard."

"I told him to let me help more. But he thinks he has to do everything for everyone himself."

"Sooner or later, he'll be asking for help. You'll see."

"Maybe. But you know Jesse. He's pretty headstrong."

"And I know you, and you are, too." Livy grinned. "Just keep offering help. He'll say yes."

She hoped her cousin was right.

Blake was sitting at the kitchen table doing homework when Jesse got home that night. It had taken him longer than usual to get The Destiny all cleaned up and closed for the night. He dropped to the chair across from Blake. "Did you get dinner?"

"I did. Evelyn gave me a sandwich, a salad, and a malt."

"Good. How was your day today?" It still amazed him that he could sit here with his *son* and talk about his day.

"Well… I kind of have a date." Blake glanced up with a sheepish look on his face. "I asked Angela, just like you said. Well, not exactly like you said. I blurted it out when Jeanie came over and asked me—more like *told* me—to take her to the Sandcastle Festival. So I said, no, I was going to ask Angela. And Angela was sitting right there next to me. And I'm such a goof. Saying it like that. But Angela said yes."

Jesse grinned. "You might as well learn early

that dealing with women gets complicated and rarely works out like you planned."

"I'll say. It was all so awkward. And Jeanie was so mad. She called us all losers and stomped away."

"So, maybe she got the hint that you're not interested in dating her?"

"Yeah, she did. But I didn't want to make her mad or anything."

"She'll get over it soon."

"I hope so." Blake leaned back in his chair. "So is it this complicated between you and Heather, too?"

Jesse closed his eyes for a moment, remembering his conversation with Heather this morning. Complicated? Yes. He opened his eyes and nodded. "It is. A bit. Everything is new right now, you know?"

"Like finding out you had a kid? And then having him live with you?" Blake grinned.

Jesse smiled. "Like that. But I'm glad it happened." He chewed his lip. "So... sometimes when I'm working late... do you think you'd want to have dinner with Heather? She offered."

"Sure, I'd like that."

That would make Heather happy. And he

wanted her to be happy. It was just the coordination of everything in his life right now that he was kind of struggling with.

"Jesse?" Blake looked at him.

"Mm-hm?"

"You don't have to worry about me. I'm old enough to get my own meals. I can get all around town—everything is walkable. I have my job to earn money to spend."

"I feel like I'm walking a tightrope trying to balance everything." Giving brutal honesty here.

"Then… don't. If some things fall between the cracks, it's okay. I was a kid with a single parent before. I know how hard it is with you balancing things. I didn't mean to make your life harder." Concern settled on Blake's features.

Jesse shook his head. "You made my life so much better. That's all that's important."

Blake's concern turned into a smile. "Mine's a lot better, too. So quit worrying so much about me."

But that was much easier said than done.

CHAPTER 10

Emily met Angela at Barbara's Boutique after school the next day. She was so excited to help Angela—it was all she could think about the whole day. They went inside and Margaret greeted them. Emily remembered asking, when she was about eight, why it was called Barbara's if Margaret ran it. Her mom said that a Barbara had opened it years ago, back in the 1920s, and it had kept its same name through the years. Just another charming quirk of their small town.

"Margaret, you know Angela," Emily said.

"Of course, Charlene's girl."

"We're going to browse around for a bit."

"Sure. Let me know if I can help."

Emily led the way toward the back of the

store, thrilled to have this chance to help Angela. Maybe with some new outfits, she'd feel more confident.

Angela followed behind her. "My mom was so excited when I said I wanted to go shopping. She's always offering to take me, but I don't like to shop much. I don't know how to pick out clothes that are... right. But... I want to wear something that will make me look... I don't know. That fits me better. Jeanie did call me a loser yesterday."

"Jeanie called all of us losers. She was just jealous Blake is taking you to the festival instead of her." And Angela was *not* a loser. Nor were she and Blake. Jeanie was such an annoying twit.

Angela didn't look totally convinced.

"Leave it to me. I'm an expert shopper. I'm warning you now, though, I'm a bit opinionated in my choices. I took Jesse shopping for school clothes when he first came to town. I'm pretty sure I overwhelmed him."

"You took him shopping, too?"

"I did. So you've been warned."

"That's okay. I trust you."

Emily sorted through the racks, selected an armful of outfits, and sent Angela to the dressing room. Angela came out time after time, showing them off.

"That one is nice. Do you like it?"

Angela nodded.

"Good, because we're only going to get clothes you like, too. Not just me. Get clothes that make you feel special. Figure out what you like, your style."

"I'm not sure I have a style."

"Don't worry, we'll figure it out."

Angela headed back in for another change of clothes and they continued picking out outfits.

"That one is not for you. Ugh."

"It's pretty horrible, isn't it?" Angela agreed and disappeared again.

"Oh, that one brings out the blue in your eyes."

"Too baggy."

"Oh, don't you love that one?"

They finally ended up with a stack of clothes for school and a specific outfit for the festival. A cute pair of shorts, top, and sandals.

"I can't thank you enough. And look at all the clothes I have for school, too." Angela looked at the pile, a stunned expression on her face.

Emily was having so much fun. She grabbed a couple of the bags of clothes. "So... now we're going to go next door to the beauty shop and look at their makeup section."

"I don't really do makeup." Angela's eyes widened and a half-frightened look settled on her face.

"I know. We'll just get a few things. Like some eyeshadow. Maybe a bit of blush. How about mascara?" She rushed to reassure Angela, not wanting to stop the momentum they had going with this transformation.

"I... don't know."

"Come on, let's go see."

They went in next door and Sally, the owner, came over. "Can I help you girls?"

"We're going to get some makeup for Angela. Nothing fancy. Just a bit to sparkle her up. She's got a date with my cousin."

"I can help with that."

Sally chose various makeup for Angela to try. When Sally was finished with her, Angela stared into the mirror at the makeup counter. "I can't believe I look like this. And it doesn't even look makeup-y."

"You look great." Emily smiled with satisfaction.

"I have time to trim your hair if you'd like," Sally offered.

"Do it, Angela. Sally is a wizard with haircuts."

Soon Angela's hair was styled in a cute cut. "Wow, I can't believe how I look." Angela's eyes sparkled with excitement. "It looks so different, but I love it."

"It's an easy hairstyle to keep up with. Not much fussing around with it," Sally said.

Which was exactly the style that Angela needed. "You look great. Really great."

They thanked Sally and walked outside. Angela's expression brimmed with gratitude. "How do I thank you for all of this? I feel... different. Good different."

"You don't have to thank me. I had a great time. I love doing stuff like this."

"I feel like Cinderella. Like you've transformed me. But not too much. Still, it feels so... well, I don't feel so ordinary anymore. You're really good at picking clothes out. I love what we found."

"You were never ordinary. But you do look great, and I can't wait to see you tomorrow at the festival. Blake said you're meeting him at the cafe booth at noon?

We're both working the morning shift there."

"I'll be there. I'm kind of nervous, though."

"Don't be. Blake's a great guy. He's your friend. Don't let a silly term like date mess that up."

Angela pursed her lips, then nodded. "I guess you're right."

Emily laughed. "Of course I'm right. I'm always right."

CHAPTER 11

That weekend the weather outdid itself for the Sandcastle Festival. Evelyn worked the cafe's booth with Emily and Blake for the morning shift. They did steady business with people grabbing her cinnamon rolls or sandwiches or slices of pie.

At noon, Angela Healey came up to the booth. Evelyn hid a grin as Blake stared at her, his eyes wide.

"Uh, wow. Angela, you look... uh... nice." Blake kept staring.

Emily jabbed him in the side with her elbow. "Really smooth, cuz."

"Hi, Blake. Emily. Mrs. Carlson." Angela's face flushed a rosy blush color.

"Blake, why don't you go ahead and walk

around with Angela? Livy will be here soon to help us."

"Yeah, we'll be fine. Go." Emily grinned.

"Uh… okay." Blake walked out of the booth. "So, you ready?" he asked Angela, still staring at her with a bit of an awestruck look on his face.

"Yes." Angela's cheeks darkened a bright red.

"Go. Have fun," Emily said.

The pair walked off into the crowd. Emily turned to Evelyn. "Boys are so silly sometimes, aren't they?"

She laughed. "They can be."

"I thought he was going to keel over when he saw her. She looked great, didn't she?"

"Livy said you took her shopping?"

"I did. Had the best time."

"She looked very pretty."

Just then Livy and Heather came walking up. Heather stared off after Blake and Angela with a smile on her face.

"Your reinforcements are here," Livy said, coming around the back of the booth with Evelyn and Emily.

Heather finally tore her gaze from Blake and Angela and joined them behind the booth. "I told Livy I'd help her here this afternoon. Mom, you should take some time to walk around the festival."

"Oh, I couldn't leave."

"Yes, you could," Livy insisted. She placed her hands on Evelyn's shoulders and turned her around, tugging at the apron ties at the back of her waist.

"But…"

"Look, here's Rob and Violet." Livy turned her around again and smiled, lifting the apron from around Evelyn's neck. "Rob, I was just saying that Evelyn should take a break and go walk around the festival. You guys could go over to the picnic basket auction. It starts at twelve-thirty."

"What's that?" Rob's forehead crinkled in confusion.

"They auction off picnic baskets. It's for charity. Evelyn has a basket entered in it. Whoever wins the bid on her basket has a picnic lunch with her."

"You do?" He turned to her.

"Yes." Of course she did. It was for a good cause. She'd planned on popping over there at the end of the auction and hoping that whoever won her basket would do a quick picnic break with her so she could get back to the booth.

"And take your time. Go see the sandcastles, too."

Livy was making it hard to say no. Especially since she stole her apron.

"What do you say, Evelyn? Should we head over there?"

She nodded, unable to come up with any reason not to. And it might be fun to see the bidding...

Rob's eyes lit up. "Well, let's go see this auction then. Violet, want to come see it?"

"I think I'm going to grab one of these cinnamon rolls, then head over to the arts and crafts section. You two go on without me. I'll catch up with you later."

Evelyn turned to Livy. "You sure you don't need me here?"

"I'm positive. Go."

"Here, take this beach blanket for your picnic. I brought it for later, to hang out on the beach with friends, but you can use it now." Emily shoved a brightly colored blanket into her arms.

Violet stayed at the booth, chatting with Heather and Livy, as she and Rob headed toward the gazebo where the auction was being held.

There was a lot of good-natured teasing as the picnic baskets were auctioned off. The Keating brothers bid against each other for Margaret's basket. Ethan outbid everyone trying to win Melody's basket. When the bidding started on her basket, she was surprised at the response. Five men, including Rob, bid against each other.

He leaned close to her. "I guess your cooking is legendary." He held up his hand again. "Forty dollars."

One of the Keating brothers raised his hand. "Fifty."

Rob looked at her and grinned. "It's for a good cause, right?" He turned toward the auctioneer. "Two hundred."

The other men shook their heads as she stood there with her mouth open. He'd paid *two hundred* dollars to have a picnic lunch with her.

"All righty, then. Come get your basket." The auctioneer nodded toward Rob.

Rob went up, claimed the basket, and returned to her side, a self-satisfied smile on his face. "So, where do you want to picnic?"

"You just paid two hundred dollars."

"Yep. Worth every penny."

She shook her head. "I think you're a bit crazy."

"Maybe." He shrugged. "I guess I'm just competitive. I like to win."

"Okay, how about going out to the beach? There are palm trees along the edge we can sit under. We could see how the sandcastle competition is coming along."

They walked across a wooden walkway and dropped down to the beach. Rob spread out the blanket under a tree and they both sat down. She opened the basket and started bringing out the meal.

"Wow," Rob said when she'd finished laying out the spread.

She really hadn't known what to pack, so she'd chosen plump fried chicken pieces, a container of slaw, cheese and crackers, a bowl of sliced fruit, and a thermos of sweet tea. Oh, and two pieces of peach pie.

"I didn't know how to keep the ice cream frozen or I would have added that, too."

"This is the best picnic I've ever seen. And probably the largest."

She blushed at the compliment. "Dig in."

They ate their lunch and watched the sandcastles being built near the water.

"This sandcastle building looks like serious business," Rob said.

"It is. There's a trophy for the winner each year. Some of these people come year after year to compete."

She leaned back on her elbows after a bit, more than full, and watched the competition.

"This was all good but I can't eat another bite. I did manage to finish my pie, though." He grinned as he, too, leaned back on his elbows. "It was a nice lunch. And nice company."

"Thank you." She shifted slightly and looked at her watch. She could probably stay a *little bit* longer. She was having such a nice relaxing time. Which was highly unusual for her. She usually worked long hours and went home and crashed. She settled back comfortably to just… enjoy herself.

Heather stood and stretched, grateful there was finally a break in the steady flow of people to their booth. Livy grabbed a bottle of water. "Want one?" She held one up for her.

"Sure. Thanks." She reached for the bottle, screwed off the top, and took a long swallow of the refreshing water. She'd forgotten how tiring it was working for the cafe. She needed to remember that before she volunteered again. And wear more sensible shoes. She looked down at her flip-flops, then at Livy with her sensible flats that had some support in them. "So... what do you think about my mom and Rob? Think there's something going on there?"

"I'm not certain. Seems like there's a spark. But I'm not sure Evelyn is ready for anything more than just friendship."

"No, probably not. She's still adjusting to single life."

"She seems really happy these days though, doesn't she?" Livy asked.

"She does."

"Hi, Livy." Charlene Healy waved as she walked up to the booth. "I hear your daughter took my Angela shopping."

Livy set down her water bottle and went up to the counter. "She did."

"I can't thank her enough. I've been trying to get Angela to go shopping for... well, forever. She hides in those baggy clothes. But the things that Emily picked out are so cute. It was so kind of her to take the time to do that. Angela even had on a bit of makeup when she left the house today. And her haircut? *So cute.* Emily accomplished everything that I've never managed to make happen."

"She and Blake headed out together to browse around the festival." Heather came up beside Livy.

"Ah, yes. Your Blake. It's her first date ever, and she was so excited." Charlene's eyes sparkled with pleasure. "I love seeing her this happy. What more could a mother ask for?"

What more could a mother ask for? Heather smiled back at Charlene, feeling like she was finally part of the secret mother society.

Livy looked over and grinned. "Great, feeling, huh?"

"Yes. Yes, it is."

Emily wandered around the festival, looking for some friends to hang out with. She ran into Blake and Angela at the funnel cake booth.

"Have you tried these? They're great." Blake broke off a piece of the funnel cake he was sharing with Angela. "I've never had one before and Angela insisted I had to try it."

"You've never had a funnel cake? You poor, deprived boy. They're great, aren't they?" She debated ordering one for herself, but she'd munched on a cinnamon roll at the booth while she worked, and she really had her heart set on a fish taco.

She frowned when she saw Jeanie approaching on the arm of Markus, the captain of the football team. Jeanie had dated him a few years ago and then announced to everyone that she dumped him. Guess she changed her mind.

"Angela, look at you," Jeanie said, her voice laden with disbelief. "What happened to you?"

"Knock it off, Jeanie." Blake stepped forward and cut her off.

She didn't take the hint.

"I mean... well, she usually dresses so... drab... and out of fashion."

"Jeanie, back off." Emily stepped up with Blake.

"What? I'm just telling the truth. She wears baggy clothes and—"

"Seriously, Jeanie. Just go away. You're being mean." Emily was so over Jeanie. *So over her.*

She glanced back at Angela, who stood

there with a shocked expression… that suddenly turned to anger as she stepped forward.

"You know, Jeanie. I really don't care about your opinion." Angela hurled the words at her.

You go, girl.

Jeanie's mouth dropped open in shock. "I— Like I said, I was only saying the truth."

"I can't believe we were ever friends." Angela's eyes flashed in anger. "What happened to you?"

"We were never friends." Jeanie shook her head and frowned. "Never."

"Sure you were, in grade school," Emily corrected her with a sickeningly sweet, ever-so-innocent smile.

"I don't remember that." But it was clear Jeanie was lying.

Markus looked a bit stunned with the conversation, and he frowned at Jeanie for a long minute.

"Markus, let's leave these losers and go hang out on the beach."

He looked down at Jeanie's hand on his arm and plucked it off like an unwanted piece of lint. He shook his head. "Now I remember why I broke up with you before."

Emily bit her lip to keep from gawking at

that little revelation. Really, it wasn't even all that surprising that Jeanie had lied about who broke up with who.

"You haven't changed a bit. You're still... impossible. You still go all mean girl. I'm done. I'm out." He turned to Angela. "I'm sorry, Angela. And you look great, by the way."

With that, he turned and strode away, leaving Jeanie standing there, her face a crimson mask of fury. She whirled around at Angela. "See what you did?"

"She didn't do anything. You did." Blake slid his arm around Angela. "This is all on you."

"You guys won't get away with this. You're still all losers." Jeanie gave them all an angry glare, spun around, and hurried off.

Then, as she crossed the distance, she met up with Kade Perry. Jeanie paused and said something to him. He laughed. Then she promptly took his arm and they walked off.

Emily stared at the couple. Perfect. Jeanie and the boy known for his troublemaking. What a pair. It appeared it didn't take her long to get over Markus.

"Look at her. She just hooked up with Kade. Those two together are trouble with a capital T. At least Markus came to his senses." Emily turned to her friends. "And Angela! You were impressive. Magnificent. Stunning. Standing up to Jeanie like that."

"I'm done with her. I don't care what she says anymore."

Emily grinned at Angela's growing confidence. "You're right. *No one* should care about what Jeanie Francis thinks or says about anything."

"I hope she thinks we're not worth her time and leaves us alone." Blake's forehead creased as he watched Jeanie and Kade.

"Between Markus dumping her—evidently for the second time—and Angela standing up to her, I'm sure she'll steer clear of us." At least she hoped so. Jeanie had an annoying habit of causing trouble when she didn't get her way.

CHAPTER 12

Rob walked Evelyn back toward the cafe's booth. She'd spent a good hour with him before he could tell she was getting antsy to get back to work. They lazed on the blanket and commented as they watched the growing sandcastles. He made a mental note to go back at four when the winners were going to be announced.

"I had a nice time. The picnic was great." He swung the basket—that still had lots of food in it even though he'd eaten an enormous amount—to his other hand. He didn't like it dangling between them.

"I'm glad you enjoyed it. The basket auction is always a big deal. I haven't entered a basket in years, though. Darren always insisted it was silly." Evelyn shrugged. "And maybe it is, a bit. But the proceeds always go to a good cause."

"I'm glad you decided to do it this year."

"I'm glad I get to make my own decisions now," she said candidly. "I can't believe I let myself lose so much control over my life. It slowly slipped away because it was easier to do what Darren wanted than push back."

He was surprised she was sharing this much about her life with him, but it pleased him that she trusted him enough to do so. "You seem pretty confident of yourself now. Owner at the cafe. Best cook in the state." She really was a fascinating woman. She intrigued him, and he thoroughly enjoyed getting to know her better.

"Well, it was a hard life lesson. I'm never putting myself in that position again. I like my independence. Love living alone in my apartment that I've decorated exactly how I want. I can support myself now. It's kind of a heady freedom."

He could see how happy and content she was with her life now. That was a good thing. And he always thought he was happy and content with his own life. Only now... being down here with Violet... He grudgingly admitted he liked helping her out with the resort. He enjoyed their sibling teasing. And it felt like he had a family again instead of being the loner he'd been for so many years, only seeing Violet about once a year when she'd finally coax a visit out of him.

"Mr. Bentley." Emily raced up to them, then bent over for a moment gasping for breath. "It's your sister. She fell. She's hurt. They sent me to come find you."

His heart clutched in his chest with fear. "Where is she?"

"Back there." Emily flung her arm. "By the beach."

"Go. I hope she's okay." Evelyn nodded and took the picnic basket from him.

He sped off after Emily as she led him back to where Violet was sitting at the edge of the beach, an EMT by her side.

"Violet, are you okay?" He sank onto the sand beside her. Blood covered her temple, and she looked shaken. And angry. "Vi, what happened?"

"She tripped. Landed on that." The EMT pointed to a large piece of driftwood in front of them.

"I was watching them finish that large

sandcastle." Violet nodded her head in the direction of the contest, then winced at the movement. "Wasn't paying attention to where I was going."

"I'm afraid you're going to need some stitches... and an X-ray of that arm. I'm pretty sure it's broken."

"It can't be. I don't have time for any of this."

"It's going to be okay. Don't worry." He helped the EMT get Violet up standing. "I'm going to take you to the emergency room. We'll get that cut looked at and an X-ray."

"I'll call ahead and let them know you're on your way." The EMT started gathering his things.

"Thanks for checking her out." He turned to Emily. "And thanks for coming to get me."

Violet looked a bit pale, and that worried him. He wrapped an arm around her waist. "Here, let's go." Then he froze. They'd walked to the festival, and it was clear that Violet was in no condition to walk back to the resort. "I don't have my car..." And for that matter, he had no clue where the nearest emergency room was.

"I know Evelyn drove today because she

loaded her car with food. I'll go get her and have her meet you over at the end of that street." Emily pointed to a street at the edge of the park.

"Thank you." He nodded, grateful for the help. "Come on Violet, let's get over there."

They headed toward the street and didn't have to wait long for Evelyn to pull up in her car. He helped Violet in and slid in after her. "Thanks so much for this."

"It's no problem." Evelyn frowned as she looked at Violet. "You okay?"

"Stitches, probably. And maybe a broken arm. How am I going to paint all those cottages with a broken arm? And it's my right arm. And, of course, I'm right-handed." Violet grimaced.

"Don't worry, sis. I'll paint." He couldn't stand to see the pain etched on her face.

"You can't do everything. It would take forever. And I don't have the funds to pay someone to do everything." Violet sighed. "I'm so annoyed at my clumsiness. This is such lousy timing."

"It's going to be okay, I promise." He'd work night and day if that's what it took. He wanted to erase the troubled look on Violet's face. Take care of her. He was her big brother. It was his job to protect her. That's what big brothers do.

Evelyn parked the car near the emergency room, and the two of them helped Violet inside. After they took Violet's information, a tech came to take her back to an exam room. "I'll wait here," he said as they rolled her away in a wheelchair. "I'm not going anywhere."

Evelyn led him over to some chairs in the waiting area and sat down beside him. "She'll be okay." She gently rested her hand on his arm.

He stared at the hand as worry raged through him. "I know. It's just… I can't stand to see her like that."

"They'll get her all fixed up. They have great doctors here."

"I appreciate the ride. But I don't know how long this will take. You should get back to the festival." Though he was grateful for the company.

"I'm not going anywhere, either. I'll wait with you, then I'll drive you home. Emily said she'd stay at the booth and help Livy and Heather. Blake offered to help, too."

"You've got a great family."

"You do, too. And she's going to be fine. You'll see."

Evelyn tried to keep him occupied as they waited. After an hour, he took to pacing the floor. Finally Violet was wheeled out to them, a bandage on her forehead and a cast on her arm.

"She needs to take it easy for a few days. And she's had some pain meds. She'll be a bit unsteady," the nurse said to him.

Violet looked up at him with a weak smile. "See? All better."

His heart thumped in his chest. She looked weak and fragile... and a bit out of it.

Evelyn drove them home and helped him get Violet inside. Violet looked down at her clothes, covered in blood. "I'm going to change."

"Here, let me help you," Evelyn offered.

He sent her a grateful look. Like she hadn't already done enough.

Fifteen minutes later Evelyn returned. "I got her changed. She said she was tired and climbed into her bed. You should check on her every so often though."

"Oh, I will." He might just camp out at her bedside. "Truly, I can't thank you enough for all your help."

She touched his arm again and he felt an instant connection with her. A bond forged by her helping him, being there for him, a stranger to her town.

"It was no problem. What are friends for?" She slipped outside, and he watched as she pulled away.

Friends.

Were they friends? Had they moved past the acquaintance stage? No time to sort this out now. He headed for Violet's room and found her sound asleep. Just what she needed. He settled into a chair in the corner of the room. There was no way he was leaving her side.

A nagging crick in his neck brought him out of a light, dozing sleep, and he opened his eyes.

"Hey, sleepyhead. I thought I was the one who got hurt." Violet was sitting up in her bed, propped up by her overabundance of pillows. She'd always had that. About twenty pillows on her bed. She always insisted she needed that many. This time he noted they were all the same bright colors like she wanted to paint the cottages.

He shoved the sleep away and got up from

the chair. "How are you feeling?" He searched her face, still seeing signs of pain.

"Got a heck of a headache and my arm aches, but I'll be okay."

"Can I get you anything? Something to eat?"

"Maybe just a cup of tea. I still feel a bit woozy."

He hurried to the kitchen to make the tea and heard a knock at the door. He opened it to see Evelyn standing there with a basket in her hands.

"I made you two some dinner. Just sandwiches. And some soup, if that sounds better to Violet." She grinned. "And some muffins, and some pie, of course. Hoping something of that will tempt Violet to eat a few bites. I tend to over pack on picnics, don't I?"

"You didn't need to do that. You've done so much already." But he was grateful and took the overflowing basket from her.

"I'm glad to help."

"She just woke up and I'm making her some tea."

"How's she feeling?"

"Pretty sore. Says she has a headache."

"I bet. That was quite a gash on her forehead."

"I'm going to make her take it easy for a few days. Not that it'll be easy. She's so determined to finish the renovations and get the resort open." And get some income coming in, though he didn't mention that. He'd seen Violet's spreadsheets, and she was hitting the end of her money to invest in repairs.

"Hopefully she'll be much better soon. Although I'm sure the broken arm will slow her down."

"I guess I'll add painting the cottages to my list of things that need to be done before she opens." Along with fixing two more wooden porches, replacing a set of stairs, new plumbing fixtures for a handful of the bathrooms and kitchens. Oh, and replace a few windows that were cracked, and a new door for one of the cottages. The staggering amount of work that still needed to be done almost overwhelmed him.

And he really needed to get started on his next book. He had deadlines of his own. If he could come up with an idea, that is...

"Tell her I hope she feels better soon."

Evelyn gave him a friendly smile and a little wave as she turned and walked back to her car.

She drove away down the rutted dirt driveway... yet another thing he needed to spruce up. How was he ever going to get all of this work finished? Pushing away his worries, he made the tea and plated up a muffin for his sister.

He trudged to his sister's room with the tea and muffin.

"Did I hear Evelyn's voice?" Violet struggled to sit up more, then rested against the pillows lining the headboard.

"Yes, she dropped off some food. I brought the muffin, but there's soup or sandwiches."

"The muffin sounds good for now."

He handed it to her and set the tea on the nightstand beside her.

"Evelyn is nice, isn't she?" Violet asked as she broke off a piece of the muffin and popped it in her mouth.

"Yes, she is."

"You seem to see her a bunch. You do go to Parker's a lot, you know."

"Well, we need supplies."

"Like you go to Parker's every single day."

She laughed. "Sometimes even inventing things we need."

"I do not."

"Do so." She sat up and grinned. "Why don't you ask her out?"

"Because…" Why didn't he? Okay, there was the fact he was leaving soon, but would a date hurt anything? It didn't have to be anything serious. Just… go out to dinner or something. Maybe he should ask her out. But then, maybe it would mess up the easy friendship thing they had going on. He didn't want that to happen.

"Hello, Earth to Rob." Violet rolled her eyes, then grimaced. "Ouch."

"I'll think about it. Maybe."

"You should listen to me. I'm younger and wiser." She grinned.

"Eat your muffin." He let out a long sigh. "Call me if you need me." He turned to leave. The dinner basket from Evelyn was calling to him.

"Hey, Rob?"

He stopped and glanced back at her.

"Thanks… I don't say it enough. But thank you. For helping me with the resort. For taking care of me today."

"Nothing I'd rather be doing." Though,

writing his next book might be a good idea. Although there was that pesky writer's block thing going on.

"Liar."

"Okay, but really, I don't mind helping. I'm actually kind of having a good time." He turned and walked away.

"Because of Evelyn. You like her," Violet called after him in a sing-song voice.

CHAPTER 13

Donna perched on a stool in the kitchen at the cafe, sipping on coffee after the breakfast rush. Evelyn sat beside her eating a cinnamon roll.

"I hear the cook here is really good," Donna teased. "Enjoying your breakfast?"

"Very funny. I am. First chance I've had to grab anything this morning."

"So, Barry and I were out to eat last night. Went to Jimmy's. Guess who we ran into on the wharf? Mother and Ted."

"Mom and Ted were at Jimmy's?" Evelyn frowned.

Donna laughed. "No, they were coming out of Portside Grill."

"Okay, that makes more sense. I know that Mother is a bit… ah… less uptight these days, but I couldn't imagine her going to Jimmy's."

Donna grinned. "No, she hasn't changed *that* much. I'm not sure we'll ever see her at Jimmy's."

"It seems a bit strange to think of her dating, doesn't it?"

"It does. But Ted always seems happy when he's with her. Even Mother seems… I don't know… more relaxed. I was actually thinking that maybe we'd have a Parker women brunch this weekend. See if Mom would come."

"We haven't done that in quite a while." Evelyn's eyes lit up.

"I thought we could send the guys out fishing. I know Barry and Ted have gone out fishing a few times. Maybe Jesse and Blake would like to go, too. I think Austin is still out of town."

"I think this is a wonderful idea. Sunday?"

"That's what I was thinking. Let me get a hold of Mother and Livy and Heather. I'll see if I can make it happen."

"Great."

Donna slid off the stool and took her cup to

the sink. "I think I'll make that egg casserole that everyone likes."

"I'll bring something, too."

"Perfect. Now I'll call Mother. Wish me luck. I still keep expecting her to turn me down when I invite her to anything."

"Hope she says yes." Evelyn stood and took her dishes to the sink. "I've got to get back to work."

"Okay, I'll let you know."

She headed out of the cafe and over to her office at Parker's marveling that they were actually hoping their mother said yes to a Parker women brunch. Man, things were really changing these days.

Evelyn sat at a table in the kitchen totaling up the receipts from this past weekend's festival. The cafe had made a handsome profit. She was pleased. Actually, both the cafe and Parker's were doing really well since they'd expanded into the second building this year. People came into the cafe, then remembered they needed to buy something at Parker's. Customers came into

Parker's and couldn't resist the enticing aromas coming from the cafe. Livy had made a smart move buying this addition.

As if on cue, Livy came into the kitchen. "Last lunch customer gone."

"Look at these numbers from this weekend." Evelyn turned the laptop for her to see.

"Wow, that's better than I'd hoped. And Melody still had the cafe open, and it was busy, too. Did you hear Ethan won her basket and brought it here and had a picnic here at the cafe with her?"

"No, I didn't. That was sweet of him." Evelyn smiled. "Anyway, if I haven't told you lately, opening Sea Glass cafe sure ended up being a smart decision."

"What can I say? I'm a genius." Livy grinned. "And I hear we're having a Parker women brunch on Sunday. Mom said Grandmother was even coming."

"She said yes?"

"I guess so." Livy shrugged. "Oh, and *someone* needs to go out and run the ice cream counter..." Livy sent her an innocent look. "A certain Rob Bentley just came in."

Evelyn jumped up. He hadn't been into the

cafe for a few days and she really wanted to hear how Violet was doing. She didn't miss Livy smothering a grin—or trying to—as she hurried out to the cafe.

"Hi, Rob. What can I get you?" She slipped behind the counter.

"You are working today." A smile broke out on his face.

A welcoming one that truly showed that he was glad to see her. It was probably just that she was one of the few friends he'd made in town so far. That was all it was.

"I work almost every day." She smiled back at him.

"Yes, but it's nice when you work the ice cream counter and I get to chat with you. Highlight of my day."

"Your days must not be very exciting," she teased. "How's Violet?"

"She's... a handful. Grouchy. So cranky. Upset that she can't do much with just her left hand. I caught her trying to paint with her left hand... it wasn't pretty. I told her the resort would open when it opens. But I know she wants that to happen soon."

"It's probably like when we opened the cafe.

You put all this time and energy and money into it… and you can't wait for it to open and see how it does. See if it earns back your investment in money and time."

"I can only do so much, and funds are running too low to hire people, so she'll have to be patient."

She nodded. "So, what can I get you?"

"You have any peach pie?"

"We do." She wasn't going to admit to him that she'd gotten into the habit of squirreling away a piece of pie for him, just in case he came in and wanted one. "I'll get it for you."

She placed the large slice of pie with the equally large scoop of vanilla ice cream in front of him.

"I think I could eat this every single day." He patted his stomach. "Though if I keep this up, I'm going to have to start exercising."

She couldn't see an ounce of extra weight. He was in really great shape. Really great. *Oh, answer him. Don't just stare at him.* "I'm glad you like it." And she silently thanked her great-grandmother for the recipe. This recipe and so many others that she used for the cafe. She was certain it was part of the reason the cafe was so successful.

She continued chatting with Rob while he ate. An idea started to blossom as she talked to him. As soon as he left, she headed back into the kitchen. "Hey, Livy... I have this great idea and I need some help with it."

"I'm all yours."

CHAPTER 14

Late that week Rob looked up from where he was replacing yet another rotted board on yet another sagging deck to see Evelyn pulling into the rutted drive. She got out and her daughter, Heather, popped out too. Then a truck pulled in behind them and the Keating brothers that he'd met at the festival got out of it. Then a handful of other people he didn't know arrived. What in the world... He set down his tools and walked over to the gathering crowd.

Violet came out of their cottage looking as confused as he felt and stood beside him.

Evelyn looked like she was going to burst with excitement as she approached them.

"Evelyn, what's going on? What are all these people doing here?"

"We've decided to have a painting party." She tossed him a self-satisfied grin. "We're going to paint all the cottages today."

"You're what?" Violet's eyes grew wide.

"I know you got a bit sidelined with that broken arm of yours. So we decided to come help you out."

"But why?" Violet still looked bewildered.

"Because you're part of this town now. And we help each other here in Moonbeam." Evelyn looked at Violet, then back at him. "So… which one of you knows where the paint is? Let's get started."

The Keating brothers came forward. "We're great at plumbing. Point the way to any plumbing problems you have."

Heather stepped up. "And I'm an expert on trim. Just tell us what color goes where. Oh, and this is Jesse." She tugged on the arm of a man standing near her. "Jesse, this is Rob and Violet."

Evelyn motioned to the rest of the crowd. "And this is… everybody. They'll introduce themselves. And I brought extra paint brushes and rollers."

"Nice to meet you. *All* of you," he said to the large crowd, still stunned by the generosity of the town.

"I'm pretty good at carpentry. If you point me in the direction of any woodwork you need finished up," Jesse offered.

More people came up and introduced themselves, and soon Violet was in her element, directing the helpers on which cottage needed which color. Everyone got busy. He helped carry paint to each cottage, then walked over to where Evelyn was stirring the paint can with the color he called orange—*possibly* peach—but Violet insisted was coral. "I don't know how I'll ever be able to thank you for this."

"You don't have to. I just wanted to help. We all did. We want the resort reopened and we're all thrilled that Violet bought it. Murphy hadn't done a thing to update these cottages in years. Such an eyesore on such a beautiful part of the beach. We couldn't let a thing like a broken arm delay her opening."

Relief and gratitude soared through him. He'd find a way to pay her back for this kindness she'd orchestrated. Somehow.

At noon Livy came by with lunch for everyone, and people scattered around on the porches and snacked on the feast she brought. He sat next to Evelyn and tried not to stare at her while she ate. He and Violet were practically strangers to the town, and yet, she'd done this for Violet. For him. For both of them. The kindness and goodness of these people overwhelmed him. He was still a bit stunned over it all.

"Aunt Evelyn, can you come over here?" Livy called out. "The Keatings know someone they think would be great to hire for the cafe. We need more help."

Evelyn stood. "I'll be back."

She walked across to the teal cottage where Livy and the Keating brothers were sitting. At least he could tell which color cottage was which as the bright paint was put on each of them.

Violet dropped down beside him, cradling her arm in her sling. "This is amazing, isn't it?"

"It is." He still stared at Evelyn.

Violet elbowed him with her good arm and nodded toward Evelyn. "She'd probably say yes if you asked her out, you know, Robby." Violet stuck her tongue out at him like she used to do when she was a little kid, bounded back up, and headed over to the teal cottage.

By late afternoon, the cottages were all

painted. Jesse had finished repairs on all the porches and stairs. The Keating brothers had gone to Parker's and gotten new glass for a few broken windows and replaced the broken panes along with fixing the last of the cottages that needed some plumbing work. Things were starting to look up for the formerly ramshackle resort.

Evelyn came over to stand beside him as the last car of helpers pulled away. "It looks great, doesn't it? I really think Violet's idea to paint each one a bright color was brilliant. It looks so cheery."

He eyed the cottages and was surprised that he really liked how they'd turned out too. "I thought Violet was crazy when she said this is what she wanted to do. I'm more of a conservative, paint them all the same color type of guy. But I agree, it turned out really nice." He turned to Evelyn. "I don't know how I'm ever going to repay you."

"You're not. There's no repaying to do. It was just neighbors helping neighbors. You're going to have to get used to how we do things in a small town, city boy." Her eyes sparkled as she teased him.

"I'm overwhelmed by everyone's kindness."

"Don't be. We were glad to help."

Maybe he should ask her out. Just to thank her for arranging all this. Show his appreciation… That would be the *neighborly* thing to do. Of course, if he did, he'd never hear the end of it from Violet.

He gathered his courage. "So… I was wondering…"

Her phone rang, and she held up one finger as she answered it. "Okay. No, I'll be right there." She slid the phone back into her pocket. "I've got to run. Getting a rush at the cafe and one of the workers called in sick."

Disappointment swept through him. He'd hoped she could stay for a bit. Maybe have some tea. Just sit and talk.

"You were saying something?"

"Never mind. It will keep. We'll talk later."

"I'm sure we will. You know, the next time you come in for ice cream." Her gentle laughter floated across the distance as she headed to her car.

He went inside and found Violet sitting at the kitchen table, sipping iced tea. She motioned to the pitcher sitting on the counter with her good arm. He grabbed a glass, filled it, and sat down beside her.

"I think that was the most amazing thing I've ever seen." Tears started to cloud her eyes. His sister was such an easy crier. At happy moments. At sad ones. Movies. Books. You name it, she cried.

"Don't start." He frowned sternly. Not that she ever listened to him.

She dashed them away. "I'm just happy. I'm so grateful. It's turning out just like I pictured it. And now we're getting really close to being able to pick an opening date. Get it up on the website. Open up for reservation. It's becoming real, isn't it?"

"It is. And as much as it pains me to admit it to you, the cottages and their bright colors turned out really nice."

"You mean I was right, and you were— what's that word again—*wrong*?" She cocked an eyebrow.

"I didn't exactly say that."

"But… it's what you meant." She grinned, her teasing chasing away her tears.

"Well, it appears you picked a very generous town to move to."

"I did. And buying this resort was a great decision, wasn't it?" Her eyes lit up.

He loved seeing her this happy. He did. So

he just smiled, not wanting to burst her joy. He still wasn't convinced that buying this place— with absolutely *no* experience running a resort— could ever be called a well-thought-out, *great* decision. But then Vi was known for her snap decisions. Maybe, just maybe, this one might work out okay for her.

CHAPTER 15

Patricia stared into her closet late Sunday morning. Brunch with the girls. She'd normally pull on one of her well-tailored pairs of slacks and possibly a silk blouse. But the girls would dress more casually, and they'd all be sitting out on Donna's lanai. It would be hot and humid, but she vowed not to complain about the heat. Or at least try not to.

She frowned as she scanned her outfits, looking for something more casual. She didn't *do* casual very often. Finally settling on a pair of navy slacks and a crisp white shirt, she slipped the outfit on. That was the best she could do. Her meager attempt to fit in.

She added some jewelry and looked at her

reflection in the mirror. Not a gray hair was showing, and as far as she was concerned there never would be one.

It was ridiculous to be nervous about going to a family brunch, but she was. Just the girls. The Parker women. She knew they all met often, but she'd turned them down so many times, they'd quit asking her to their Parker women brunch. But this time they'd asked her and she'd accepted the invitation.

She was trying—really she was—to be more social with her family. It was hard to change from years of habit, though. Her husband had rarely had time for family functions. He was all about business dinners and events. It was easier to go along with his decisions than try to change his mind. Now that he was gone, it was hard to grasp the concept that she got to make her own decisions about where she wanted to go and who she wanted to see.

She'd never been very close to her daughters or her granddaughter. Maybe she didn't have the proper mother gene in her. But she was trying to make things better.

It was still hard to bite her tongue around them, though. They made so many choices that she disagreed with. But as Ted had pointed out when they talked about it, the girls had just as much right to be making their own decisions as she did now. Practical advice, but still hard to live with.

The receptionist called up and said her driver had arrived. She took one last look, grabbed her purse, and headed downstairs.

Evelyn helped Donna in the kitchen, getting everything ready for the brunch. Livy and Heather came in laughing and laden with the makings for mimosas.

"So, Mother really said she was coming?" Evelyn asked for like the fourth time. It still shocked her that their mother *wanted* to come.

"Hey, she's really changed since she started going out with Ted. I saw her actually strolling through the park with him the other day." Heather set the Champagne on the counter. "Since when does Grandmother go on walks?"

"I'm not sure when it started, but it has to be Ted's influence. She's not much of an outdoors person." Livy plunked the orange juice next to the Champagne. "You did tell her that we'll be outside today for brunch, right?"

"I did." Donna nodded.

"She seems different these days. Less stuffy. More… relaxed? It couldn't have been easy living with Father all those years. He was… hard. Critical." Evelyn shook her head. "It's strange to think that she's dating *your* father now, Donna. What a twist of fate."

"I'm still not over the shock of finding out that Ted is my father. But I've enjoyed getting to know him better. We had dinner a few times. Barry and I had drinks out on the porch at The Cabot Hotel one evening with him and Mother. It's all kinds of new and strange. I've seen more of Mother in the last six weeks than I have in the last six *years*."

The doorbell rang, and Donna hurried off to answer it, returning with Patricia.

"Hi, Grandmother. I'm making mimosas. Want one?" Heather offered.

"That sounds lovely."

"I thought we'd have drinks on the lanai, then I'll take up brunch. The casserole still needs another fifteen minutes or so." Donna snatched a tea towel from her shoulder, folded it carefully, and placed it on the counter. Then glanced at their mother as if waiting for her to correct her towel folding or complain about moving outside.

But their mother just carried her drink and followed Heather and Livy out the door. Evelyn couldn't help but notice that she sat rather rigidly in her chair, though. She was dressed more casually than usual, which was nice. Donna, Livy, and Heather were dressed in a mixture of shorts, a sundress, and capris with a t-shirt. Her mother *almost* fit in. She certainly was trying. Evelyn would give her that much credit.

"So, Mother. Livy said she saw you at the park with Ted." Evelyn tried to pull her mother into their conversation.

"Yes. Ted and I take walks almost every day. It's nice to get out and get some fresh air."

Who was this woman and what had she done with her mother? "Uh… every day?"

"Almost. Unless it's raining, of course. Ted loves to take nice long walks. We started taking short ones, but…" She gave a graceful shrug of her shoulders. "I seem to be getting to where I can take longer ones with him. I even bought something called walking shoes. Not very chic, but practical."

She couldn't picture her mother in anything

but the stylish pumps she usually wore. She stole a glance at her mother's footwear. Still pumps, even for a casual brunch. At least that much hadn't changed.

"Ted seems like a nice guy," Livy chimed in.

"He's a very nice man." A delicate blush crept over her face.

Evelyn had never seen her mother like this. Never seen her—she stared at her mother as a wave of shock swept over her—her mother was *happy*. There was no other way to describe it. Happy. She was certain she had never, ever seen her mother happy.

She glanced over at Donna, who gave her a knowing smile. Donna had noticed it, too. Evelyn looked around at all of them, and love swirled through her. She was so lucky to have this family. And so much the better if her mother was softening toward all of them.

As if reading her mind, Donna raised her glass in their traditional toast. "To the Parker women."

"Oh," her mother said, a smile widening as she raised her glass, as if surprised to be included.

"Oh, let me get a photo of this." Evelyn propped her phone across from them.

"To the Parker women," they all toasted as the photo captured the moment.

After brunch, the driver dropped Patricia off back at Sunrise Village. It rather annoyed her that she needed a driver now, but she'd had a couple of fender benders, and she was trying to convince herself that a driver was a luxury she could afford, not some no-driving-allowed sentence.

She walked into the lobby, thinking about what a good time she'd had today. And she was slightly taken aback at the realization. She'd enjoyed the company. Enjoyed the conversation. Though, she'd been right in thinking that it would be hot and humid. It had been beastly hot.

The girls had talked about Parker's, and Heather had shown some new sketches she was working on. They talked about Barry, and Austin, and Jesse. And she even talked a little bit about Ted. What a surprise he'd been coming into her life again.

"Hi, there." Ted smiled at her from his seat

in the lobby as if summoned up by her thoughts.

Her heart quickened at the sight of him. "I thought you were out fishing today?"

"Got back a bit ago. I got cleaned up and thought I'd come wait for you and see how your first official Parker women brunch went."

She sank onto the chair beside him. "It went just fine. I was nervous at first. That's silly, isn't it? I mean they are my family."

"It's not silly if that's how you felt. And as you've told me, you haven't been very close to them in recent years."

"I haven't. I don't know how I let Nelson keep me so distant from their lives. And then I got used to it being that way. I can't blame the girls for pulling away from me, either. I was rather... judgmental."

"But things are better now."

She let out a long sigh. "Oh, but how I wanted to tell Livy that her shorts were really too short for a woman her age. A woman of any age."

Ted laughed. "But you didn't."

"I didn't. And I didn't tell Donna that she really needs a haircut. Maybe even a new style."

He laughed again. "You are the most charming mix of correctness and… candor."

She'd take that as a compliment. Probably.

"And for the first time… I really felt included. Like I was really one of the Parker women."

He reached out and squeezed her hand. "And I'm very, *very* happy for you."

CHAPTER 16

Jesse stood on the top deck of The Destiny, enjoying the breeze. They'd had a morning breakfast cruise out to the gulf and were just about to head back in, though that would take them a couple of hours. As much as he loved the dinner cruises, the breakfast ones were fun, too. And today was a perfect day out on the water. Light breeze. Minimal waves. Sunshine. He stood by the railing and enjoyed watching the boat cut through the sea.

His cell rang, and he grabbed it from his pocket, frowning when he didn't recognize the number. "Hello?"

"Is this Jesse Brown?"

"It is."

"This is Mrs. Grimshaw." He frowned. The principal from the school.

"Is something wrong?"

"I'm afraid there is. You need to come in and talk to us. There's been… a problem."

"Is Blake okay?" Fear swept through him and he clutched the railing.

"Yes, he is. But you'll need to come get him."

"Why is that?"

"He's been suspended."

His mouth dropped open, and he swung the phone away from his ear and stared at it for a moment. He must have heard wrong. He shoved the phone back to his ear. "What did you say?"

"He's been suspended. We'll discuss it when you come in."

"I'm two hours out to sea." He now glared at the water stretched before him.

"Ah… that's unfortunate."

Jesse's mind raced. "Let me see if I can send his mother."

"We just have you listed as the legal contact on his enrollment form."

"Well… it's complicated."

"I'm afraid we can't let someone else pick him up without permission."

"I'm giving you my permission," he said in exasperation.

"Written permission."

"Fine. Give me your email and I'll send it to you."

"I guess that will work," Mrs. Grimshaw said grudgingly, not very thrilled that he'd suggested an end-run around her rules.

He wanted to reach through the phone and strangle her. Small town. He knew she'd heard the talk and knew that Heather was Blake's mother. And he'd heard gossip about how this new principal they'd hired a few years ago was a stickler for details. Unbending. He just hadn't ever thought he'd actually be dealing with her.

He grabbed a pen from his pocket and wrote her email address on his hand. "Heather will be there as soon as I can find her."

"Call me back if you can't locate her. Then... well, I guess he'll just have to sit here in my office until you can get him."

She hung up on him with a click before he could ask again what had happened. He raced to the bridge, grabbed a piece of paper, and wrote out his permission for Heather to pick up Blake. He signed it, took a picture of it, and sent it to Mrs. Grimshaw. Then he clicked on Heather's number.

It rang once.

Twice.

Come on, Heather, I need you. Blake needs you.

"Hello?"

"Heather. Thank goodness. I'm out on The Destiny. I need you to go to the school and get Blake."

"Is he hurt?" Panic rose in her voice.

"No. No, it's not that. Mrs. Grimshaw called, and she said he's been *suspended*." Even saying that sounded ridiculous to him.

"Suspended? Blake? No. What for?" The shock in her voice matched exactly how he felt.

"At this point, I have no idea. But I'm two hours out to sea and can't get him. Will you?"

"Of course." She paused. "But will they let me?"

"Yes, I sent my permission."

"Okay, I'm leaving right now."

"Call me as soon as you find out anything."

"I will."

"And tell him I'll be there as soon as I can." Jesse clicked off the phone and turned to Leo. "Turn her around and pick up the pace a bit. I need to get back to Moonbeam."

He stared out the window, regretting that *this* particular day he'd be so far out when Blake needed him. And what in the world could Blake have done to get suspended? He was not a troublemaker. He was a good kid. A great kid.

He shoved his hands into his pockets, impatiently staring at the water slipping past them. To him, it seemed like they were going in slow motion.

Heather tapped her foot, sitting on the hard chair the receptionist had told her to take. Blake was nowhere to be seen. She sat there and watched the minutes tick by on the large, industrial-looking clock on the wall. Did every school in the United States have those? She'd swear the second hand was going slower and slower in its infuriatingly lazy loops around the clock face. At this rate, Jesse would be here before she even got a chance to see Blake.

She could *not* think of a reason that Blake would be suspended. Not Blake.

After what seemed like an eternity, the receptionist finally told her she could go into Mrs. Grimshaw's office. Heather rose, squared her shoulders, and went in to see what this mess was all about.

Blake sat in a chair against the far wall. Relief swept over his face when he saw her. "Heather," he said softly.

She nodded to him, searching his face for some... clue. "Jesse is out at sea. He's coming."

Blake nodded, his face a mix of miserable and... mad?

"Take a seat." It was more of a command from Mrs. Grimshaw than anything else.

She took a seat across from the principal. "What's going on?"

"Blake has been caught plagiarizing. We take that seriously here at Moonbeam High. We have a strict code of ethics. Plagiarism is always a week's suspension."

"What? Blake wouldn't plagiarize." She turned to Blake. "Blake?"

"I didn't." His face was a stony mask of anger and denial.

"It's hard to deny it. Here's his paper he wrote for Miss Brady's class. She said it seemed different from his other papers, so she put it through the plagiarism detection program." She handed her his paper.

She looked at it. Saw the paper, his name on it. Saw the big red F.

"That's not the paper I wrote. That's not the paper I turned in." Blake's voice held an edge of panic.

"What do you mean?"

"Mrs. Grimshaw showed that to me and I told her that's *not* the paper I turned in."

"You'll have to come up with a better excuse than that." Mrs. Grimshaw turned her stern face to Blake. "You can't deny it. It has your name on it. And there's no other paper turned in with your name."

"I can't explain it, but that paper you're holding is not my paper."

"But, Blake—"

Mrs. Grimshaw didn't let her finish. "You'll need to take him home now. He's suspended for five school days. I'll arrange for his assignments. You can come back and pick them up. He'll need to do all of them—with his own work this time—before he can return." Mrs. Grimshaw frowned, her lips pressed into a hard, thin line. "I don't know what his prior schools were like, but we consider this a serious infraction of our rules here at Moonbeam High. And this will go on your *permanent record*."

The way she said permanent record sounded ominous and scary. What exactly did that mean? And her look was actually kind of scary... no wonder the rumors circulated about her.

"Blake, let's go." She stood.

"But what she says I did... it's not true."

"We'll talk about it at home. Let's go." Blake trudged behind her the whole way out to the car. She was at a loss. She couldn't imagine that Blake would copy someone else's work. He was a good student. But she didn't want to be one of those parents who was always making excuses for their kids. Letting them get away with things. Still... this didn't sound like him. But then Mrs. Grimshaw had held the evidence in her hands. Her thoughts banged back and forth like a loose hurricane shutter in the wind.

They drove to Jesse's cottage, and Blake didn't say a single word. They went inside and Blake dropped his school bag to the floor, went and grabbed a soda, and sank onto a chair in the kitchen. She sat across from him.

"Okay, talk to me. Tell me what happened. The truth."

"I told the truth. I didn't copy off someone. I didn't plagiarize. I wrote a really good paper. I turned it in. Set it on Miss Brady's desk. That paper you saw? That wasn't what I turned in. I *didn't* cheat." His words were filled with defensiveness.

"I believe you, son." Jesse appeared in the doorway.

Blake got up and walked over to Jesse, and Jesse wrapped him in a hug. "I believe you. You've always told the truth. No reason to think you'd start lying now. Let's figure out what really happened."

Heather stared at Jesse. His absolute belief in Blake. The confidence he had in him.

And she suddenly felt like such a failure. *She* should have been that confident. Believed in him. Not worried about what kind of parent she'd be. Just… ugh. She'd failed Blake when he needed her. The first chance Jesse had given her to be there for Blake… and she'd failed him.

CHAPTER 17

Jesse let go of Blake, and they sat down at the table with Heather. "Now, tell me what happened."

"I got to Miss Brady's class today, and she told me I had to go to see Mrs. Grimshaw. She wouldn't tell me why. When I got there, she had this paper—and it had my name on it—but it wasn't the paper I turned in. I swear."

"I told you I believe you. I do. Go on." Jesse nodded. He did believe Blake, and it surprised him how *strongly* he believed him. He couldn't imagine Blake cheating like this. *Plagiarizing.*

"Mrs. Grimshaw wouldn't listen to me. Said I was suspended. But I didn't do it."

There was a knock at the slider behind

them, and he turned. Emily. He got up and let her in.

"I heard what happened. I came over on my lunch break. Blake would never cheat. He wouldn't."

"Thanks, Emily. I didn't. But I have no idea how this could happen."

"Well, let's *prove* you didn't." Emily plopped down on the seat next to Blake and dumped her schoolbag at her feet.

Blake's eyes lit up. "I wrote it on my laptop. It's saved online to SupremeMax Drive. I printed it out from there. I can show you what I wrote." He wrestled his laptop out of his backpack and flicked it on. He clicked some keys and brought up his account. "See, here's what I wrote."

Emily leaned closer to the screen.

A deep frown settled on Blake's face. "It's… not here." Panic started to spread across his face. "It's gone… and that paper. The one Mrs. Grimshaw had? It's… here."

Jesse frowned. "How could that happen?"

"I don't know."

Emily leaned forward. "So what's your password to SupremeMax? Could someone have figured it out?"

"My password is..." Blake closed his eyes, then opened them, a spot of red growing on his cheek. "Angela." He shook his head. "I mean, I didn't think anyone was interested in what I was writing or putting in there. It's just papers and stuff. It's the service the school suggested we use." He slammed his hand on the table. "How could I have been so stupid?"

"You're not stupid. But I admit that's a dumb password. Too easy to figure out." Emily shook her head.

"So someone hacked into Blake's account?" Heather frowned.

"Looks that way." Jesse was worried now. How would they ever prove that Blake hadn't turned in the fake paper? "Who would want to do this to you?"

"Oh, that's easy." Emily's face hardened into an angry glare. "Jeanie Francis."

Emily hurried back to school after her lunch break. It seemed like every third kid stopped her in the hallway between her afternoon classes to ask about Blake. Which, technically, no one should know why he was suspended... unless someone was spreading the rumor.

And she had a pretty good idea who that person was.

After her last class, she went outside and there was Jeanie standing with Kade and a bunch of his friends, laughing. Anger swelled through her as she stalked over to the group and stood right in front of Jeanie, glaring at her. "I know you're behind this, Jeanie Francis."

"I'm sure I don't know what you're talking about," Jeanie insisted, but a smirk covered her face.

"So it looks like your cousin got caught cheating, huh? That's too bad." Kade laughed. "Gosh, I'm so sorry about that." Sarcasm dripped from his words.

Before she had a chance to correct the jerk, Angela came hurrying up and stood beside her. Her face was pinched in fury. "Jeanie, this is low. Even for you. I know you did this. Blake would not copy someone else's work. He's not like that."

"Of course he did. Mrs. Grimshaw had the paper to prove he did. The evidence wouldn't lie, would it?" If it was even possible, Jeanie's smirk widened, threatening to split her face.

"I'm going to prove he didn't do this." Angela crossed her arms, staring daggers at both Jeanie and Kade. "And then, whoever is behind this will pay the price."

"Right." Kade tossed out a hard, mean bark of a laugh. "You just go ahead and prove that."

"Come on, Kade. I'm tired of these... *losers*." Jeanie took Kade's arm, and they walked away with his friends, all of them laughing.

Angela turned to her, bright spots of red highlighting her cheeks. "You know Blake didn't cheat, don't you? You believe him."

"Of course I do." She sighed. "But someone hacked his SupremeMax Drive account, too. This fake paper is on the drive and the one he wrote is gone."

"Oh, no. How did that happen?"

"He used a *really* simple password." She rolled her eyes. "*Angela*."

"Oh... no." Her blush threatened to take over her whole face now.

"Oh, yes. My cousin is really smart... except when he isn't."

"So how can we prove he didn't really do this?" Angela frowned.

"I have no idea." Anger and panic engulfed her at the injustice of everything.

Blake didn't cheat, but they had no way to prove it.

Heather sat at Jimmy's, waiting for Livy. She'd made these dinner plans yesterday, but now what she really wanted was to stay with Blake. But Jesse decided to take him out on The Destiny's dinner cruise, so both of them headed out for the evening. And going out on The Destiny would hopefully keep Blake busy and lift his spirits some. Maybe.

He was so upset that he couldn't prove that he was telling the truth. Though both she and Jesse believed him. So did Emily. They just needed proof to show the school. But it appeared that wasn't going to happen.

Livy slid onto the chair across from her. "Sorry I'm late. Oh, my gosh. Emily told me what happened to Blake. That's terrible."

"It is. And to make matters worse, when I first heard what happened, I was uncertain. Blake said he didn't do it, but I was afraid I'd be one of those enabling parents. You know the ones. The parents who fix everything for their kids and never make them take the consequences. I kept second-guessing myself." She took another sip of her beer. "Not Jesse, though. He immediately believed what Blake was saying. I should have been like Jesse."

"Hey, parenting isn't easy. We try and do the best we can. And those hovering, enabling parents drive me crazy. Their kids grow up thinking they can get away with everything." Livy shook her head.

"But even though I believe Blake is innocent, I don't think there's any way we can prove the truth."

"Prove the truth about what?" Austin walked up to their table.

Livy jumped up and threw her arms around him. "You're back. I didn't think you were returning for days."

"I missed you." He wrapped his arms around Livy and held her close for a moment. "I went by Parker's and Donna told me you two were meeting here for dinner."

"Sit. Join us." Heather motioned to a seat.

"You sure I'm not interrupting a girls' night?"

"Not at all."

"How's your mom doing?" Livy asked as she and Austin sat down.

"She's holding her own. Still weak. But not getting worse. They have her on some new meds that seem to help her pain but make her groggy, so she doesn't like to take them."

"I'm sorry, Austin." Livy took his hand in hers.

Austin nodded, and he and Livy ordered drinks when the server came by.

"So… you were saying you couldn't prove something?" Austin leaned back in his chair.

Heather told him the whole story about Blake.

"And Emily is certain Jeanie Francis is involved somehow. She's been hanging out with Kade Parry, who's quite a troublemaker." Livy reached for the drink the server brought and took a sip. "Ah, needed this. It's good."

Heather leaned forward on her elbows, scowling. "And Mrs. Grimshaw—wow, she is *scary*—said it would go on his permanent record. Do you think colleges will know that he got suspended? This is such a mess."

"I think some admission applications might ask. I'm not certain." Livy frowned.

"I'm not either. It's not something I thought I'd ever have to deal with." She sighed as she leaned back in her seat, wanting to pound the table in frustration.

Austin frowned and rubbed his chin, his forehead creasing. "So you said that Blake used SupremeMax Drive? Hm..."

"What are you hm-ing about?" Livy elbowed him.

"There has to be some kind of redundancy. Some kind of backup. Let me do some checking around." Austin nodded slowly. "I might be able to find something. No promises though. And I know a guy that works for SupremeMax Drive Corporation. I'll call him tomorrow."

"That would be great. Thank you for at least trying." A small glimmer of hope flickered in Heather.

"I'll try. Let me do a bit of research into the service and I'll see what I can find. I'll need his password."

"I'll get it for you when they get back on land tonight. I know he changed it to some impossible combination of unrelated letters, numbers, and symbols."

"That's good he changed it. Never use your girlfriend's name." Austin shook his head. "You'd be surprised at the passwords my clients tell me. ABC. 123. The name of their dog or cat."

"I'm sure he's learned his lesson about passwords. I hope so." Heather looked over at Austin, the computer wiz, and hope stirred. Maybe she could make up for not immediately believing him like she should have. Like Jesse did. And maybe, just maybe, they could find a way to help Blake out of this mess.

CHAPTER 18

By Wednesday Heather had almost given up hope. Austin hadn't called saying he'd found anything, and Blake was getting progressively more sullen. She'd been coming over and making his lunch and showing her support.

She puttered in the kitchen, cleaning up the lunch dishes at Jesse's after Blake left to go work at Parker's. She turned as Jesse entered the kitchen.

"Did I miss Blake?" He frowned. "I wanted to get here before he left for work."

"You just missed him."

"How was he today?"

"He's... quieter now. Subdued. He didn't

even perk up much when Angela called him. I'm worried."

"I'm sure it's hard to be accused of something you didn't do and not be able to prove it. It was hard enough starting a new school where almost every kid grew up together here in Moonbeam."

"Emily told Livy that all the kids were talking about Blake's suspension. It's going to be so hard for him to face that when he goes back next week."

"I know." Jesse plunked down in a kitchen chair.

Her phone dinged, and she looked at the text message. "It's Austin. He found something. He wants to come over."

"Tell him yes." Jesse's eyes lit up. "I hope whatever he found can help Blake."

She finished the dishes, then paced the floor, waiting for Austin to arrive. Jesse sat at the table sipping some iced tea, lost in thought.

Finally Jesse jumped up at the sound of a knock. She hurried to follow him to the door. Austin and Livy stood there on the front step. She grabbed Livy's hand and tugged. "Come in."

"Austin, what did you find?" Jesse led them into the cottage.

"It's such good news," Livy grinned. "Show them."

Austin took out his laptop and snapped it open. The screen brightened, and he pointed at it. "I found out how to get to the backups. Luckily this service keeps deleted files for thirty days. See these files? Here's Blake's original file."

Livy thrust a paper toward them. "We printed it out for you."

"And here is when it was deleted and the new file uploaded. And it gives me the IP address—that's like the location—of where the upload occurred. It was uploaded from the school late Friday afternoon."

"That would have been *after* he turned in his paper." Heather frowned.

"And Blake couldn't have done it. He was working at Parker's at that exact time. We have tons of people who can say they saw him." Livy flung her arms wide triumphantly.

"I've done a screen print of the file time stamps." Austin handed them a page. "And if this isn't enough for the principal, I'd be happy to go to the high school and login in front of her and show her all this. Or here, I'll show you how to bring all this up for her on your laptop."

"Austin, I can't thank you enough." She threw her arms around him and hugged him.

"I'm glad I could help."

Jesse pulled out his phone and dialed. "I'd like to speak to Mrs. Grimshaw. This is Jesse Brown."

His face clouded. "I see. Well, I'd like an appointment first thing in the morning." His scowl deepened. "Tell you what. I'm going to show up first thing and I'll wait until she *does* have time to see me." He clicked off the phone.

"She won't see you?" Heather asked.

"The very important Mrs. Grimshaw is very, very busy. I swear I'll sit there all day until she'll see me," he said fiercely. "I'm not letting this go on any longer."

"We need to tell Blake." Heather grabbed Jesse's arm. "Let's go to Parker's and tell him right now."

Jesse frowned. "Let me talk to Mrs. Grimshaw first. See how this plays out. It's been such an emotional roller coaster for him this week. Let me see if we can present him with a done deal."

"Then I'll bring breakfast over tomorrow and wait here with him until you get back."

"Hopefully you won't have to wait all day," he muttered.

CHAPTER 19

The next morning Jesse arrived at the school as soon as the doors were unlocked and stalked down the vinyl-clad—and very ugly—hallway to Mrs. Grimshaw's office. The lights were out, so he took a seat in a chair in the reception area. The receptionist came in and barely acknowledged him with a tiny—no, *minuscule*—nod.

Well, okay then. It was going to be like that. He was the interloper, the parent the principal didn't want to deal with. Ah, but she would have to. Or he'd go to the school board. Anyone who would listen to him.

An hour later—an hour spent tapping his foot and getting angrier by the minute at the injustice that had been done to his son—Mrs.

Grimshaw came in. He jumped to his feet. "Principal Grimshaw, I need to talk to you."

She frowned. "I didn't see you on my schedule."

"No, you didn't. Your receptionist wouldn't give me an appointment. It won't take long, but I have something you need to see."

"I know every parent wants to believe their child, but I've been in this business long enough to know when there is no way a student is telling the truth."

He stood in front of her. "And that's where you're wrong. Blake is telling the truth. And I can prove it."

She frowned, shaking her head. "Five minutes. That's all the time I have." She turned and strode into her office, her heels clicking on the tile, and flipped on the lights.

He followed her and placed his laptop on the desk. "Here, look at this."

He logged in like Austin had explained to him, and the backup files for Blake's account appeared on the screen. "Here are the backups for Blake's SupremeMax Drive account. The account the school has the students use." He stabbed a finger at the screen. "See this file? The date and time stamp on it? That's the original paper he wrote." He clicked on it, and it popped open on the screen.

Mrs. Grimshaw put on reading glasses and leaned closer, frowning. "I don't understand."

"*This* is the paper he wrote." He handed her a printout of it. "And now, look at this." He pulled up the plagiarized paper. "See when this was uploaded? Same time that Blake's paper was deleted. And... it was late Friday afternoon. From the school's computer system. Blake was working at Parker's then. He couldn't have uploaded it. Here's a printout for you of all the info and the IP addresses."

She leaned back and stared at him. "So you mean someone deliberately did this to Blake? Why?"

"We have a theory but can't prove it. And we sure aren't going to accuse anyone without proof. We've seen firsthand what false accusations can do to a person." He gave her a hard stare. "But if you can find out who was logged into the school's computers late Friday afternoon, then maybe you can find your proof."

"I'll talk to our head of technology. See what he can find out." She rose from her seat. "I'm sorry this happened, Mr. Brown."

"I'm not the one you should be apologizing to." He turned to leave. "I'm going to go get Blake now and bring him back to school."

"Please tell him to stop by my office when you get here."

"We will. I'll be with him." And Blake better be hearing a heartfelt apology from Mrs. Grimshaw or else. He didn't know what the else was... but he was in full-out protective parent mode now, and Blake deserved so much better than the blows life had been throwing at him.

Jesse burst through the front door of his cottage. "Blake, you here?"

"In the kitchen," Blake called out.

Heather and Blake sat at the kitchen table, eating some of Evelyn's cinnamon rolls. He strode over to the coffeepot, poured a mug, and sat down. "So, I have news. I'm taking you back to school."

"But Mrs. Grimshaw said I was suspended for a week."

"That was before we proved you didn't do what she said you did."

"But how?" His eyes widened, and he jumped up. "How did you manage that?"

"Austin helped us." Heather grinned.

"You knew about this, too?"

She nodded.

"Austin got into the backup system and found your original paper, along with the fake one uploaded in its place. I turned in a copy of your real paper, by the way. The fake paper was uploaded from an IP address at the school and your original paper deleted at the same time. And when all that was happening at the school? It just happens to be when you were working at Parker's. Mrs. Grimshaw is going to look into who might have done this."

"You found out all of this? You did this for me?"

"Of course. I believed you. We just needed to find a way to prove it."

"Austin overheard Livy and I talking about it and said he'd look into it. And he found the proof." Heather beamed with happiness.

Jesse's face probably looked just the same. He was so thrilled to be able to prove Blake was telling the truth all along.

"I need to thank Austin."

"And you can. But first, I'm taking you back to school. No need to miss any more classes."

"I'll be ready in five minutes." Blake sprinted out of the kitchen.

He looked over at Heather. "You okay?"

"Of course," she said, her voice husky. "I'm just really happy that this worked out."

He got up and pulled her to her feet, wrapping his arms around her tightly. "It did work out. We make a pretty good parenting team, don't we? Considering we're just newbies at the job."

"We do." She smiled up at him, then pressed her cheek against his chest.

He stood there holding her, feeling like things were finally falling into place in his life. And he planned on enjoying every minute of it.

Emily stood impatiently outside Blake's classroom. Why hadn't the teacher let them out when the bell rang? She tapped her foot, staring at the clock across the hall, ticking away the seconds. It was lunchtime, and she had much to talk to Blake about. The rumors were already flying around about him being back at school.

Finally the door swung open, and the students streamed out. She caught Blake as he came through the door. "Blake."

"Hey, Emily. Surprise." He flung his arms out in front of him. "I'm here."

She grinned. "And it's a good surprise. My mom told me this morning what Austin found. That's awesome."

She paused for a moment to send dagger-filled glares at a couple of kids walking past them, staring at Blake.

"I can't believe he figured all that out."

"Austin is a wiz at computers." She tugged his arm. "Come on, Angela is going to meet us in the lunchroom."

Blake looked so relieved. She'd been worried about him. He'd withdrawn so much in just a few days and hardly said anything at work yesterday. But now he could put this behind him. They walked into the lunchroom and Angela waved to them.

They hurried over to join her.

"Blake, I'm so glad to see you here at school. Emily told me what Austin found. So Mrs. Grimshaw couldn't still keep accusing you."

Blake grinned at Angela and sat down beside her, taking her hand. "Hi."

Angela squeezed Blake's hand and the now-familiar dopey smile settled on her face.

Emily plopped down across from them, smothering a grin. She took out an apple from her backpack and bit into it, then paused when she saw Jeanie and Kade headed their direction.

"Watch out. Here comes trouble." She nodded toward the duo approaching them.

"Well, that was a short suspension. I thought that cheaters usually got a week's suspension." Jeanie tossed her curls over her shoulder. "Why are you back so soon?"

"Because we proved he didn't cheat. But you knew that already, didn't you?" She glared at Jeanie and Kade.

A quick look of panic crossed Jeanie's face. "What do you mean you proved he didn't do it?"

"I bet you'll find out." Blake gave Jeanie a knowing look. "I bet both of you find out."

"How—" Kade started to ask but stopped when the computer teacher walked up to them.

"Jeanie. Kade. You need to come with me to Mrs. Grimshaw's office."

A look of total panic—not just a hint—settled on Jeanie's face. "I don't understand…"

"Come with me. Now. Both of you."

Jeanie sent Blake one more lingering look filled with alarm and trailed behind the teacher out of the lunchroom.

Emily sat back in her chair. "So, it looks like they might have found out who did that to you." She grinned at Blake and Angela.

"It looks that way, doesn't it?" Blake smiled back at her.

Relief blazed through her. Blake had been vindicated. Their lives could get back to normal. Maybe things could all settle down now.

Angela looked at Blake with adoring eyes. Blake had his love-struck goofy expression back. Looks like life was already back to normal for those two.

CHAPTER 20

The next morning Emily hurried up to Angela and Blake, who were standing at Blake's locker. "Hey, did you hear the news?"

"About Jeanie and Kade?" Blake grinned. "We did. Two-week suspension for both of them. And no afterschool activities for the rest of the semester. That should keep them away from us for a while."

"Jeanie is going to be so mad when she gets back to school." Angela's forehead creased. "I'm a bit worried about how she might retaliate."

"Yeah..." Blake's grin turned into a scowl.

Emily lounged against the locker and grinned, savoring the moment. She swung her arm wide. "So... you haven't heard *all* the news."

"What?" Angela frowned, looking a bit worried.

But then, it was smart to worry about Jeanie. And yet… she had news to share. "The Jenkins twins came into the cafe last night when I was working." She paused for dramatic effect.

"Come on, Em, just tell us."

"Okay, okay. Here it goes. Jeanie Francis's father got transferred. I kid you not. They're moving away." She paused again and couldn't contain her grin. "Next month."

"Really?" The worry seemed to melt right off his face. "She's moving?"

"The Jenkins sisters are the best source of information in the town. So, yes. It's for real. They even heard Jeanie's mother talking about not sending her back to school after the suspension. She thinks the school is being unfair to her poor, unfortunate daughter. And that Kade is the one who got her into trouble. Her Jeanie would never do anything like this. And she wants her precious, not-her-fault daughter way far away from Kade."

"She's really moving away?" Angela stood there with a stunned expression. "We don't have to worry about more problems with her?"

"Nope. The girl is history."

Angela gave a delighted laugh and threw her arms around Blake. "This is such great news, isn't it?"

Blake looked about as stunned with Angela's spontaneous hug as he had about the news Jeanie was moving. Suddenly Angela jumped back as if only just realizing what she was doing.

Emily swallowed a grin. "Well, I should be getting to class. Just wanted you two to hear the good news."

She turned and headed off down the hallway, no longer hiding her grin. Her cousin might be in over his head with his relationship with Angela. But she didn't think that was necessarily a bad thing.

CHAPTER 21

Rob sat at the kitchen table in the owner's cottage staring at his sister's computer. "You'll need a new site. And you need a way for people to book reservations online. This current site is... pathetic." He pushed the laptop toward Violet.

"But I don't have the funds to pay for someone to redo the website and put in a reservation system." Violet shoved the laptop back at him.

"You can't have a phone call be the only way to book a reservation. You'd need someone answering the reservation line all day and evening. You need an online booking system. And the website looks like it was made fifteen years ago."

"It probably was." Violet shrugged.

"You need this. And… *I'm* paying for this." He gave Vi a hard stare, hoping she wouldn't argue with him.

"No, you're not."

Short-lived hope. "Yes, I am.

"Not."

"Come on, Vi. Let me invest in this. I'm coming around to the idea that this really was a good investment for you. Moonbeam is a good place for you."

"And how about you? You like Moonbeam, don't you?"

"I… do." He nodded.

She gave him her wheedling smile. "You should move here, too."

How had they gotten from him paying for the technical work they needed to talking about him moving here? He narrowed his eyes at her. "How about you let me pay for Austin Woods to help us with the technical stuff—"

"And you'll move here?" she interrupted him.

"I'll *consider* it." He shoved the laptop back to Violet.

She stared at it, drumming her fingers on

the table. "Okay. You can pay for it. But that's all. You've already done so much for me."

"Hey, what are big brothers for?" He laughed. "And one more thought. How about renaming the place? Give it your own spin."

She chewed her bottom lip, and her face crinkled as she gave it some thought. "That's not a bad idea. It's actually a great idea. I'm surprised I didn't think of it myself." She sent him a wide grin. "I'm usually the one with the great ideas."

"Right." He rolled his eyes. "Anyway, you think of a name, and we'll see if Austin can get us a domain for it."

"You know, for an author, you know a lot about business."

"Hey, I still have to market my books. Run my author business. I don't just sit and pound out words all day."

"Speaking of which, I haven't seen you write since you got here."

"I'm… taking a little break."

"You're stuck again, aren't you?" She sent him a knowing glance.

He let out a long sigh. His sister knew him so well. Probably too well. "I am. Have been for months. It's like no idea seems big enough, or good enough for my next book."

"You'll figure it out. You always do."

He hoped his sister was right. "Hey, since you insist you're the one that always has the great ideas, maybe you can come up with an idea for my next book."

"Maybe I will." She got up from the table, slid the laptop towards him, and sent him a smart-alecky grin. As she headed outside, she paused in the doorway. "And I also think I had a great idea when I told you to ask Evelyn out."

She disappeared, and he sat at the table, staring at the empty doorway. Maybe his sister was right. Maybe that was a great idea.

Evelyn had gotten used to Rob coming in for ice cream most afternoons and looked forward to chatting with him while he enjoyed his treat. Today was no exception, and she waved to him as he entered the cafe.

He settled onto a stool across from her. "Vanilla malt today. No... do you have any peach pie?"

"I do. Coming right up." She grabbed the

pie she'd saved for him—not that he would ever know that—and placed a large scoop of vanilla ice cream on top. She slid it across the counter and smiled when he dug into it. The man did love his peach pie and ice cream.

This almost daily ritual was beginning to feel... comfortable.

He continued with his pie, taking his time eating it. "So today Violet agreed to me hiring Austin to update her website and put in a reservation system."

"That's great."

"I'm a bit surprised she agreed to it. She wants to do it all on her own. But I don't mind investing a bit in it. I want her to be a success with this."

"I'm sure she will be. I drove by the other day. It's really starting to look great. I see you got the drive all filled in with crushed shells."

"That drive was terrible. It about shook you crazy to drive over it. It's much better now. Anyway, we're getting closer. I think Violet said she wants to have the grand opening in about six weeks, so I really want to jump on this website redo. She's also going to rename the resort."

"What a good idea. A fresh start. Then

people won't tie it in with Murphy's rather... um... *lackadaisical* approach to keeping up the resort."

"You mean his total disregard to repairs and updates?"

She laughed. "That too."

He finished the pie and pushed the dish away from him. "That was great, as usual."

"Glad you enjoyed it." She set the dish in a tub under the counter and reached for a cloth to clean the counter. She thought he was getting ready to leave, but he still just sat there on the stool.

"So...I was wondering something." He paused and studied her face.

"Yes?"

"I wondered... I mean, I was wondering if... you'd like to go out to dinner with me." The last words came out in a rush.

She paused, cloth in hand, and stared at him, shocked. Had he just asked her to dinner? But she was *just* getting comfortable with this afternoon chat thing. She swallowed. "I don't know. I haven't really dated in... well, forever. Not since I was a young woman. I recently divorced and I'm still getting used to that. I don't think I'm ready to date."

"How about if it's not a date? Just two friends going for dinner. I'll take a friendly meal with you. Besides, you arranged for all those people to help us paint and do repairs on the cottages. It's the least I can do to thank you." Hope sparkled in Rob's eyes.

"Can I pay for my own meal?" She narrowed her eyes, watching for his reaction to her request.

"I should pay after all you've done for us."

"No, I want to pay my own way."

"If it makes you feel more comfortable." He nodded agreeably.

It would. Because then it wouldn't be a date. It would just be friends meeting for dinner. But she still wasn't certain that this was a good idea. She liked the comfortable little same-same life she was building for herself.

He continued to look at her with his eager half smile.

Before she could overthink it anymore, she blurted out, "We could try. I'm not making any promises. But a dinner out sounds nice. Where do you want to go?"

"Your choice."

"How about Jimmy's? It's at the end of the wharf. Casual."

"How about going tonight before you change your mind?" Rob winked.

"I... okay." If she didn't think about it— dwell on it—everything would be okay. Though, she did want to run home and change for their just-friends dinner.

His eyes widened in surprise at her answer, and a grin spread across his face. "Perfect."

"I'll meet you down in the lobby of my apartment at six." There, that gave her some feeling of control. Picking where they'd meet. Choosing the time.

"I'll be there."

He grinned the whole way out of the cafe, and when she saw him through the front window, the wide smile was still etched on his face.

What had she done? Was she really ready for this? But it was just friends meeting for dinner. She didn't have to overthink it, did she?

Of course, she did.

Donna walked over to her. "You okay? You looked... flushed."

"I'm fine. No, I'm not."

"Which is it?" Donna's forehead wrinkled.

"I'm fine. I think. I'm meeting Rob for

dinner tonight. We're going to Jimmy's. Just as friends, of course."

"Of course." Donna nodded, struggling to hide a smile.

"Don't smile. Just friends." Evelyn scrubbed the counter vigorously, then paused. "Do you think... do you think this is okay? I'm not really ready to date. I'm just getting used to being single. And... I like it. There's a lot of freedom being single. I'm not even sure if I'm ready to have a guy friend."

"Why don't you just meet him for dinner and have a good time? See how it goes. You don't have to do it again if you don't want to. Or you can if you have fun. Lots of choices here, Evie."

"You're right. I should go and have fun. He is easy to talk to. And I haven't gone out to dinner in forever."

"There. See. You made the right choice." Donna took her by the shoulders and spun her around. "So, go back to the kitchen and wrap up what needs to be done. Tell Melody I'm here if she needs help with the dinner rush tonight. Then go home and change. I don't think you need to wear your Sea Glass Cafe t-shirt to dinner."

Evelyn laughed. "No, I probably don't." She hugged Donna. "Thanks."

"Hey, you already had it sorted out. In your over-thinking kind of way."

She laughed and hurried off to the kitchen, mentally ticking off clothes in her closet and trying to figure out what looked like a casual outfit for meeting a friend.

CHAPTER 22

R ob was surprised that Evelyn agreed to a dinner out with him. Even if he had to agree that she'd pay her own way, which he wasn't thrilled with, but if it made her feel more comfortable, so be it. He grabbed a quick shower and changed into slacks and a collared short-sleeved shirt.

He walked into the kitchen, and Violet looked up from the table. "You look nice. Where are you going?"

"I'm going to have dinner with Evelyn."

She grinned. "It's about time. Took you long enough to ask her out on a date."

"It's not a date. She insisted on paying for her dinner. Just friends meeting up to eat. I said it was to pay her back for arranging all that help for us, but she insists on paying her own way. So it's not really a date." Though, to be honest, he wished it was one.

"I see." Violet looked doubtful. "Whatever you say."

"I'm just glad she agreed to go with me."

"That Austin guy called this afternoon. Said you'd called him. We're set up to meet with him tomorrow morning. He's coming here."

"Perfect. Hopefully, it won't take long to get everything set up and you can open up for reservations."

She frowned gloomily. "But I need a name for the resort before then..."

"Better put on your thinking cap and come up with one."

"But a name seems so... permanent. Important. A huge deal. Can you think of any ideas?"

"Colorful Cottages. Moonbeam Cottage Resort. Seaview Resort. Seashell Resort." He spouted names off the top of his head.

"Wow... how do you do that?" She scribbled the names down on a piece of paper. "I've been doing internet searches and I've only come up with two names. And I don't really like either of them."

He laughed. "You've never been good with names. Remember your first cat? You couldn't think of a name you liked, and the poor thing was called Cat for its whole life."

She scowled. "Yeah, I remember. And this naming business is hard. Really hard."

"You'll think of the perfect name. I have every faith in you." Okay, that might be a bit of a lie. She really did have a hard time with names...

She let out a groan. "I hope you're right."

"I'm always right," he grinned.

"Well, I—your *wonderful* sister—was right about you asking Evelyn out." She threw him a triumphant grin. "I told you she'd say yes."

Not willing to concede she was right in the sibling battle of teasing, he glanced at his watch. "Oh, look at the time. I should leave so I'm not late."

"Have a good time." She sent him a sassy look before bending her head back down over her paper, scribbling ideas on it.

He just hoped she'd decided on a name before he got home tonight, or he knew he'd be in for a long night of brainstorming with her.

~

Rob arrived promptly at six and Evelyn met him outside the lobby, finally dressed after changing clothes half a dozen times. But the simple flowy navy skirt and navy and white striped top had finally won the battle over her indecision.

"Hi." His gaze swept over her from head to toe. It was just a quick look, but she felt it like a physical weight. He was probably surprised to see her in something other than the Sea Glass Cafe t-shirt and slacks that she wore most days at work.

"You're right on time." She nervously adjusted the silver bracelet on her wrist.

"I'm a prompt kind of guy." He grinned as they started walking.

They strolled along and chatted, their steps in sync. *Casually chatted*. Like casual friends. Everything was going to be just fine.

When they got to the wharf, Jillian and Jackie came bustling up to them. Well, maybe not *perfectly* fine.

"Good evening, ladies," Rob welcomed them with a friendly smile.

"Well, Rob and Evelyn. I didn't know you

two were dating. Did you know that, Jackie?" Jillian asked.

"No, no… we're not dating. Just going to dinner at Jimmy's," she quickly assured them.

"Really. You Parker women are always insisting that going to dinner isn't dating. Livy said that about Austin and look at them now." Jackie grinned knowingly and nudged her sister. "They're engaged."

"No—it's just dinner," she insisted again, then glanced over at Rob, who looked amused. "Just dinner," she repeated.

"Whatever you say, dear." Jillian shared a conspiratorial glance with her twin. "Have a good time at… *dinner.*"

"Thank you, we will." Rob winked at them and they both beamed in return.

"Don't encourage them," Evelyn said as they continued down the wharf. "They'll be spreading rumors all over town. You said this was only dinner."

"And it is," Rob said, his eyes twinkling.

She looked ahead of them and saw her mother and Ted headed toward them. Her mother waved. Was everyone in Moonbeam at the wharf tonight?

"Hello, Mother," she said as they got closer.

"Hello, Evelyn." Her mother eyed Rob. "And this is?"

"Rob, this is my mother, Patricia Beale. And this is Ted Cabot."

"Nice to meet you." Rob gave them a friendly smile.

"I didn't know you were dating someone, Evelyn." Her mother's voice held a slight accusation at being surprised. Like she hadn't been included on the inside track.

"Oh." She pointed back and forth between herself and Rob. "We're not dating. We're just going for dinner." Couldn't people eat a simple meal together without the whole town jumping to conclusions?

Her mother ran her gaze up and down Rob, obviously sizing him up. Just great.

She was way more nervous about them meeting Rob than he seemed about meeting them. *Why was she nervous? She was just having dinner with him!*

"Yes, we're headed to Jimmy's for dinner," Rob said.

Please don't ask them to join us. She sent her pleading thought winging toward him. Smashing toward him. *Please don't.*

"Ah, we had an early dinner at Portside Grill," Ted said.

Relief swept through her. They'd already eaten. Perfect. She was certain she wasn't up to a dinner with the four of them.

"And guess who we saw there? Darren. He was positively *rude* to me." Her mother frowned.

"I'm sorry, Mother." Though why she was apologizing for Darren anymore was beyond her. An automatic reflex, she guessed.

"And that woman was with him. The man has no shame."

"Mom, we're divorced. He can date who he pleases." And live with whoever he pleases, for that matter. Even the woman he left her for.

"Still, it's just… wrong. And she's like half his age." Her mother shook her head.

"We really should get going." She interrupted her mother's tirade about Darren. He was the last person she wanted to think about tonight.

"Yes, we should." Rob nodded. "It was really nice to meet both of you."

They started down the wharf once again, and she swore she could feel her mother's eyes boring into her as they walked away. So far, this wasn't turning out exactly as she planned.

Then it got worse when she saw Darren coming out of the trendy Portside Grill with Lacey on his arm. She gritted her teeth as he headed their way. Rob looked at her curiously as she slowed her pace and tension sparked through her.

"Evelyn, what are you doing out?" Darren threw the question at her, his expression filled with surprise.

Why ask that? Because she wasn't allowed to be out with someone? Annoyed, she put on a deliberately neutral face before she answered him. "Going to Jimmy's."

"And who is your date?" Darren eyed Rob, the disapproval clear on his face.

Not bothering to correct him because it was none of his business—and she was really tired of correcting people—she introduced Rob. "This is Rob Bentley. His sister bought Murphy's Resort. She's remodeling it and reopening. Rob is here helping her." Why was she explaining so much to Darren? "Rob, this is Darren... and Lacey." She could barely force the woman's name out between her lips.

"I would have thought someone would tear it down, not try to restore it. It's a dump." Darren's eyes held contempt at the very idea.

"My sister is doing an excellent job." There was a protective edge to Rob's voice. "It's going to be a nice little place when she finishes."

"I guess we'll see." Darren's expression showed he clearly doubted it.

Typical Darren. Opinionated. Critical. And Lacey clung to his arm like he'd disappear in a good breeze.

"We should get going." Evelyn turned to Rob. "I bet you're famished."

"That I am." He gave a brief, polite smile to the pair. "Nice to meet both of you."

They started to walk away, but Darren stepped in front of them. "It's just like you to date a common construction worker. You never could grasp what was expected of you. You never really did fit into my lifestyle."

"Goodbye, Darren." She didn't bother to correct him and explain that Rob was an author. Nor did she care about fitting into his so-called lifestyle. She sidestepped him, and Rob followed. They walked a ways down the wharf and she glanced back, making sure Darren and Lacey were headed away. Then she dropped down on a nearby bench.

Rob settled down beside her, his eyes kind and caring. "Want to talk about it?"

"That was my… ex-husband."

"I figured that much. I could feel the tension crackling between you two."

"And Lacey—she's the woman he left me for."

"Really? He left you for *her*?"

She would be forever grateful for the incredulous look in his eyes. "Yes."

"He's rather critical about things, isn't he?"

"He is. Always. Sorry about his ugly remarks about you and the resort."

"You don't have to apologize for him."

She should take those words to heart. She no longer had to apologize for Darren's nasty remarks. She needed to break the habit. "You're right."

"You still okay with going to dinner? We've had kind of a rough walk on the wharf tonight." He chuckled, but his smile was gentle, understanding.

He was always understanding. Patient. A really good guy. And she was annoyed at herself that she let Darren get to her. She rose from the bench. "Yes. Yes, I do still want to go to dinner. I'm craving a grouper sandwich and an ice-cold beer."

Rob stood. "Perfect. Let's go, then. And I think I'm ordering the exact same thing. You never steer me wrong when it comes to food."

Rob leaned back in his chair as he finished his meal. He'd been right to order the grouper. It was delicious. Evelyn seemed to relax as the evening went on, putting their run-in with Darren behind her. He sipped on his wine as Evelyn finished up her meal.

She took her last bite and set down her napkin. "So you were saying that Violet is trying to rename the resort?"

"She's having a bit of trouble. Well, lots of trouble. She's not big on figuring out names. She had a cat called Cat for its whole life. And a teddy bear named Bear, for that matter. I might have to stay here all night to avoid going home and being roped into a naming brainstorming session that might last for hours."

"Livy had a hard time naming the cafe, too. She finally decided on Sea Glass Cafe—and I love that name—but most of the town calls it Parker's Cafe. Really riles Livy. So, no matter what name Violet comes up with, the town will still probably refer to it as Murphy's Resort." Evelyn's clear blue eyes sparkled with amusement.

When she smiled at him, she had the same look of the young girl who had worked in her grandmother's store all those years ago. Not that she'd really caught his attention back then. He was more interested in sports and ice cream at that age. He just remembered she and Donna had worked there every summer when he'd come in for ice cream. Like every single day that he'd been in town. Of course, not much had changed. He was still going there almost every day for ice cream.

"What are you thinking about? You're smiling."

He looked up, startled. "Oh... I was thinking about going to Parker's when I was young. Getting my ice cream. You and Donna working there as girls."

"I don't really remember you coming in, I'm sorry."

He laughed. "It was a million years ago and Parker's was always filled with customers. I was impressed at how hard you two worked."

"We loved working in the store. We earned

our own spending money, and, well, Grandmother needed the help."

"A true family business."

"It was. Kind of. My mother never worked there. Not her thing. And then Donna took over the store after my grandparents retired."

"Did you work there after Donna took over?"

"No, not really. By then I was married to Darren and he didn't want me working at Parker's. He wanted me planning events at the country club, hosting business dinners, and getting involved in what he considered proper charities. He said he couldn't have a wife working retail." She shrugged. "And, for some reason, I let him run my life. Not too proud of it now."

He couldn't imagine her with Darren. From their brief meeting, he could tell he was a hard, critical man, and Evelyn was so kind and friendly.

"Anyway, that part of my life is behind me. I have my job at the cafe. My own apartment. I'm really proud of all I've accomplished since splitting with Darren. It might be the best thing that ever happened to me. I would have just grown old with him, miserable in my life."

"That's no way to live."

"No, it's not. And I love my job now. Cooking, coming up with new recipes to make. It's very fulfilling." She looked over at him. "Is that how you feel about your writing?"

He gave her a wry grin. "Usually. But I'm in a funk right now. A big case of writer's block. Usually I can work my way out of it, but this time it's clinging to me hard."

"What's your favorite part of being a writer?"

He thought for a moment. "One of the best things is when a reader writes me and tells me how much they enjoyed my book. How they got to escape into it for a time."

"That must be nice."

"I also love when I get really into the flow of writing and the story pours out from my fingers to the keyboard. And sometimes my characters surprise me. I'm like—no kidding—that's what happened?" He grinned.

"I read one of your books."

"You did?"

"Of course. After getting to know you, I wanted to see what kind of books you wrote. It was The Lady Under the Lake. Very good. What a twist you put at the end of it."

Her praise thrilled him. "Thank you."

The server came by. "Dessert?"

"I'll have the chocolate molten cake," Evelyn said.

She hadn't steered him wrong on food yet. He ordered the same.

They finished their meals—she paid for her own—and they left Jimmy's. He made a mental note to bring Violet here. She'd love it.

They strolled along the sidewalks toward her apartment building. All too soon, they arrived at her building. She stood under the streetlight, the soft glow illuminating her easy smile. "I had a really good time tonight."

"I did too." So good that he didn't want it to end.

"I should go up. Early day tomorrow."

He nodded, disappointed she didn't ask him up to her apartment. He'd hoped for a drink and some more talk. He *almost* asked her, but didn't. Shouldn't push his luck.

"I guess I'll see you tomorrow when I come in for my ice cream."

She laughed. "Yes, I'll see you then."

She slipped inside and he continued to stand under the lamplight. Soon a light turned on and shone through the window on an upper floor.

That must be her apartment. A shadow moved across the window before the blinds came down.

Feeling lonely—which was ridiculous—he headed back to the resort, hoping against hope that Violet had already picked out a name for it.

CHAPTER 23

Early the next morning, Heather pushed through the door to the kitchen at Sea Glass Cafe, anxious to hear about her mom's date. Not that her mom had told her about the date… "Mom, I knew I'd find you here."

"Of course. Grab yourself some coffee. I have to get this new batch of peach-filled scones in the oven."

"Sounds yummy." She poured some coffee and sat on a stool by the counter, watching her mother work. "So… how was your date last night?"

"It wasn't a date." Her mother looked up quickly. "Why does everyone insist it was a date?"

"Well, I heard about it from Jillian and Jackie. Not from my very own mother."

Her mother finished the last scone and popped the tray into the oven. "We just went to Jimmy's. Very last minute. I paid my own way."

She eyed her mother. "You did?"

"I insisted."

"You're a bit of an enigma, Mother." She took a sip of the hot coffee. The cafe had really good coffee. Better than she made at her apartment. She should figure out their secret or what kind of coffee they brewed. "Did you have a good time?"

"I did. Though we ran into your father and Lacey."

"Really? I haven't seen him around lately. Figured he was out of town. Not that he's speaking to me since our last run-in."

"He was just as lovely as ever." Her mom rolled her eyes. "Insulted Rob. Insulted Violet remodeling Murphy's Resort. Just lovely."

"I hope you ignored him." She frowned. Her dad was such a jerk. She was actually *glad* her parents had divorced. And without her father calling all the shots, demanding her mother avoid all family functions, she'd gotten closer to her mom this last year.

"I try to. I admit, he still does get under my skin."

"I'm sorry. I hope running into him didn't ruin the evening."

"No, it didn't. And we ran into Mother and Ted, too."

"Busy night at the wharf. The twins. Grandmother and Ted. Dad and what's her name." She actually *knew* the girl's name but refused to say it.

"It was. I thought we'd just have a quiet dinner."

"But you still had fun, right? Enjoyed yourself?"

"I did."

"You know… it's okay if you want to date, Mom. You're divorced. You're free to do what you want."

A serious expression settled on her mother's face. "That's the thing. I don't know what I want."

"And you know what? That's okay, too. You don't have to make any decisions. Just enjoy yourself. Enjoy your life now."

Her mom patted her hand. "And I am. I really am enjoying my life now."

Heather slid off the stool. "And I'm happy

for you. But I gotta run. Oh, and next time tell me when you have a date-not-date."

She headed out the door. Things were looking up for both of them. Blake's school problems were over. Jesse was making progress on legally becoming Blake's guardian, and she had another date scheduled with Jesse this week. She'd echo her mother's words. She was enjoying her life now, too. It was funny how sometimes when disastrous things happened— like her father divorcing her mother and leaving her penniless, or Jesse finding out about Blake— those disasters could sometimes turn into blessings.

Austin sat at the kitchen table at the owner's cottage of the freshly named Blue Heron Cottages.

Rob leaned back in his chair, enjoying his sister's enthusiasm as she told the story. *And* extremely thankful she'd come up with a name on her own.

"You see. I couldn't think of a new name for the place. I really didn't want to keep Murphy's Resort. So last night I walked to the edge of the water, thinking." Violet's eyes sparkled with triumph. "And this beautiful blue heron came walking up to me. She just stood there, staring for a bit. I chatted with her for a while." Violet grinned. "Then she gave me one last look and slowly swooped off into the sky, into the sunset. It was the most beautiful thing I've ever seen. And then I knew I'd found my name for this place."

"Sounds like a fine name to me. Let me check on domains so we can get one that we can use." Austin clicked on his computer keys, searching.

They agreed on a domain name and bought it. Then Austin asked questions to get an idea of what Violet wanted for the website and showed her a few sites he thought were well done as well as the reservation system he thought she should use. They also discussed which social media accounts he would set up for Blue Heron Cottages. By the time he left, it felt like all their technical problems were solved.

Violet came back from walking Austin to the door. "The guy is a wiz, isn't he? He knows so much techie stuff."

"Seems to. You happy with everything?"

"More than happy. And that reservation

software isn't too expensive. That's good. And he gave me the friends and family discount for his work. Just because you're friends with Evelyn, I guess."

"Or because the whole town is excited that you're reopening Blue Heron Cottages and the tired old Murphy Resort will be a distant memory."

"It's really happening, isn't it?" Her eyes glistened with excitement.

And seeing her so happy made him happy, too. In spite of all his doubts, this really might have been the best decision his sister had ever made. There was something to be said about being happy with your choices in life.

He got up from the table. "I'm headed to the nursery to pick out some plantings for the courtyard. That's still on my to-do list, and I would love to check it off. Want to come along and help?"

"I sure do. I don't trust you. You keep calling the coral cottage orange. What do you know about what looks good?" She sent him a teasing grin.

"Come on, then. Let's go. Seems like your brother has a lot of work to do this afternoon."

"As much as I'd love to help you dig holes for

the plants and all, I'm afraid I can't." She patted her broken arm and grinned.

As if she would have been digging holes even if her arm wasn't broken. He rolled his eyes at her but really didn't mind the work. Maybe an afternoon of hard work would help break through his writer's block. Maybe.

CHAPTER 24

Heather spent a wonderful evening having dinner alone with Jesse at his cottage. A *perfect* evening. They moved outside after dinner to enjoy the gentle breeze.

"We should probably quit kissing before Blake gets home and catches us necking again." Jesse grinned as he pulled back, his eyes teasing.

"We probably should."

"Maybe just one more." He leaned over and kissed her again, and she grasped his shoulders to steady herself. A Jesse Brown kiss could make a grown woman go weak in the knees.

He pulled back again and took her hands in his, his eyes locking with hers, drawing her like a magnet. "There's something I've been wanting to talk to you about."

"Okay." She settled back on the glider but missed his lips on hers.

"I know we've only been *officially* dating for a little while. But you've been my best friend since we were kids. You still are. I love you, Heather Parker. I can't imagine my life without you. You make things... right. I wondered if— I mean—" He swallowed. "You probably think I'm crazy but—"

She held her breath, barely able to think or concentrate. What was he trying to say?

"I know the timing is crazy. Right in the middle of me getting legal custody of Blake and everything... But..."

"But what?" she whispered, waiting for him to finally finish a sentence.

He dropped to his knee in front of her. "Heather, would you marry me?" He popped open a ring box, and a diamond sparkled in the soft glow of the lanterns.

And her world fell into place with his words. A life with Jesse and Blake. She couldn't imagine anything better. Her heart pounded, swelling in her chest until it felt like it would explode.

Marrying Jesse.

Something she'd wanted for most of her life, even if she'd been unable to admit it to herself.

"Heather? Are you going to answer me?" His face was frozen in suspense.

"Yes, Jesse Brown. I'll marry you. You're my best friend. You've always been my best friend. I love you. And we'll get to be a family."

A wide grin spread across his face. "A family. Yes, we'll be a family. The three of us."

He slipped the ring on her finger and she stared down at it in awe. It was perfect. Simple. Understated, but beautiful. He knew her so well and she loved it.

He stood, tugged her to her feet, and wrapped his arms around her. "I think this is the happiest I've ever been."

"Me, too, Jesse. Me, too." And she pressed against him, secure in his arms with joy flooding through her.

"And let's not wait. Let's get married soon. Very soon." His eyes flashed eagerly. "Okay?"

"I'm all for that. The sooner the better." She didn't want to miss one more day with Jesse. One more day with Blake. She paused, pursing her lips. "But it will be hard to find a place at the last minute. I'm sure the pavilion at The Cabot Hotel is booked by now. And most of the usual wedding venues."

"Well, I have a great idea. If you'll agree to it." His eyes sparkled.

"What's that?"

"How about getting married on The Destiny?"

"Oh, Jesse. That would be perfect. We can get married on a sunset cruise in the harbor. That sounds wonderful."

"I'll check the schedule and we'll pick a date. You sure The Destiny is okay? I want you to have the wedding you want. A special one. The one you've always dreamed of."

"The Destiny is perfect. *Better* than perfect."

"And you can plan the wedding however you want. I'll say yes to *anything*. Everything."

"I bet that's the last time you'll ever promise that." She laughed.

"You're probably right." He grinned as he pulled her close again.

"Hey, kid in the room." Blake laughed as he came out on the deck.

Jesse pulled back from her but still held her hand, captured in his. She squeezed his hand, unsure how long they had been standing there kissing.

Jesse turned to Blake. "And you are just the kid we wanted to see."

"Why's that?" He lounged against the doorframe.

"Jesse and I have some news and I hope you'll be happy about it." She stood up and her heart sped in a rickety beat as she fought to find the right words. "Jesse and I—I mean we..." She looked at Jesse, imploring him to help her. The words were just not coming.

As usual, Jesse knew just what she needed. "What Heather is trying to say is that I asked her to marry me. And she said yes."

Blake let out a whoop. "Really? That's the best news ever." He came over to her and wrapped her in an exuberant hug.

Which was exactly what she needed. She held him tightly for a moment before pulling away and searching his face. "So you're okay with this?"

"Are you kidding? I can't think of anything better than you two getting married. Seriously." He grinned. "And I'll finally be part of a family again."

Jesse stood and came over to stand beside them. "Yes, we'll be a family. There for each other forever." He wrapped one arm around her, and one around Blake.

"Really, I'm happy for both of you. So when are you getting married?"

"We're thinking four weeks. We're getting married on The Destiny."

"I can't wait to tell Emily. She's going to be psyched, too. This is great news."

"I'm going to tell my mom and Livy tomorrow. You can tell Emily when you see her at school."

"You bet I will. This is the best news I've heard since Jesse said he was going to become my legal guardian."

"I'm hoping that part goes through soon… but then… I'm hoping that Heather and I can legally adopt you. What do you say to that?"

Blake stared at Jesse. She stared at Jesse. Her heart pounded with excitement at the idea of the adoption. She would officially be Blake's mother again. The idea filled her with so much joy she could barely breathe.

"Okay, *that* is the best news I've ever heard. For real, this time." Blake's stunned expression slowly slipped into a grin.

And Heather's heart filled with love for both of these men. For Jesse. For her son. For her soon-to-be family. Tonight would certainly be a night to remember.

CHAPTER 25

"Mom, you here?" Heather burst into the kitchen of Sea Glass Cafe first thing the next morning.

"Of course." Her mother turned, a sheet of cinnamon rolls in her hands.

"Go ahead. Put them in." She nodded toward the oven.

Her mom slipped the rolls into the oven, turned, and wiped her hands on a dishtowel. "What brings you here so early?"

"I have some news." Heather flung her hand out, showing her the gorgeous ring Jesse had given her. "Jesse and I are getting married."

"Oh, Heather." Her mother hurried over and gathered her into her arms. "I'm so happy for you."

"I'm pretty happy for me, too."

"Here, let me see the ring better." Her mom let her go and took her hand. "Oh, it's so pretty."

"It is. I just love it."

"And you've told Blake?"

"Yes, last night when he got home from Parker's."

"And I bet he's pleased."

"He seemed happy about it. And there's more. Jesse and I are going to start the process to adopt Blake."

"Heather, that's wonderful news."

Heather stared down at her hand, watching the diamond sparkle from the overhead lights. "I can't believe this is happening. It's like a dream. I'm getting everything I've always wanted."

"And you deserve it. I hope this makes you very happy."

"I'm happy, Mom. Very happy." She pulled her stare from her ring. "And now I have to go find Livy."

"Run along, then. I'm sure she'll be excited, too."

Heather hurried out of Parker's and over to Livy's house, hoping she'd be home. She knocked once and went inside, calling out her name.

"In the kitchen."

Heather hurried to the kitchen, gave Livy a hug, and pulled away.

"What has you so happy this morning?"

"Everything." She shoved out her hand.

Livy screamed. "Yes. This is the best news ever."

"I think so." Heather felt the unending smile stretch across her face.

"We're getting married in four weeks. On The Destiny."

"That will be so romantic. Sail at sunset. Get married on the harbor. That really is a great idea." Livy paused and frowned. "So... are you going to invite your father to the wedding? Will he give you away?"

Heather sank onto a nearby chair. "I hadn't really given it any thought. I don't know if I'll invite him—I sure don't want to—but he won't be giving me away. I'm going to have my mom walk me down the aisle."

"That's perfect. Fabulous idea. Now we need to plan everything." She grabbed a pad of paper. "Evelyn will plan the food, of course."

Heather nodded.

"We need flowers. Oh, and invitations like *really* quick. And a dress. You want to go shopping right now?" Livy jumped up from the table.

She laughed. "Right now? Really?"

"Well, a dress is kind of important. And you have your own style."

"I was thinking of wearing Grace's dress. The one your mom had altered and wore for her wedding. It just seems like a family tradition by now. Though, I was thinking of adding a teal ribbon around the waist and wearing teal shoes."

"A bit of teal, of course. And we'll get some flowers to match. I think that sounds great. We should go try it on and see if it needs altering. We can get Ruby over on Belle Island to re-alter it if it needs it."

Livy collapsed on the chair across from her. "I'm just so happy for you."

"And you're okay with me getting married before you? I mean, Austin did ask you to marry him first. Before Jesse asked me."

"Don't be silly. I don't care if your wedding is before mine. I'm happy for you. Happy for both of us." Livy grinned. "And you know what? I'm going to double task. I'm going to pick out invitations and flowers for my wedding while we're looking for you. See, I'm clever like that."

She laughed and stood. "Okay, then. What are we waiting for? Let's go to the florist."

"Hey, Emily. Wait up."

Emily turned from closing her locker to see Blake jogging up the hallway to her. She glanced at him and laughed. "So, what's up? I can tell something is, just from your face."

"Yes, something is up. Guess what? Jesse asked Heather to marry him and she said yes."

"He did? That's fabulous." Emily twirled around, grinning. "Like great. Really great. Wow, another Parker woman wedding." She hugged him for a second and stepped back.

"And they are getting married in four weeks."

"No kidding? Four weeks? Well, I'm sure my mom will help her plan everything."

"Heather was going to tell Evelyn and Livy first thing this morning."

"Mom is going to be thrilled. She's always said that Heather and Jesse were destined for each other."

"Well, I guess it's fitting that they are getting married on The Destiny then."

She laughed. "Very fitting."

"And I have more news. Almost bigger than that."

She eyed him suspiciously. How could anything top that? He'd just found out his parents were getting married.

"They... they are going to adopt me. Both of them."

She let out a little squeal, and she wasn't really the squealing kind. "No kidding. That's great."

"We're going to officially, legally, be a family. I mean, I know the legal stuff takes time, but it will happen."

"I'm really happy for you, Blake."

"And Jesse is really happy about the wedding. He was whistling in the kitchen this morning. Poured himself two different cups of coffee."

"*Jesse*... huh? Are you ever going to call him Dad?

"I don't know. I've thought about it. But... well, he's never asked me to call him that. I just don't know."

She pinned him with a stare. "Do you want to call him Dad?"

"I... I do. But then... there's Heather."

"You mean your *mom*? The one who is marrying your dad?" She rolled her eyes.

"I don't want to do anything to mess up things between them. I don't want them to feel all weirded out if I call Jesse Dad. If I do that, I should call Heather Mom... but I haven't gotten to know her as well as I have Jesse. And well, there's my Mom—the one who raised me. I know she's gone now, but it will be hard to call someone else Mom. See how it gets complicated?"

"I think if they're getting married and plan to adopt you... you should consider the whole Mom and Dad thing. But I get how it would be hard with the Mom thing. But at least consider it."

"You're right. It's just that so much has happened in the last year. So many changes."

"Like finding out you have the best cousin ever?" She grinned.

"Yes, like that." His face broke into a grin.

"Have you told Angela yet?"

"Not yet."

"Go find her and tell her. She'll be really happy for you." She shooed him away.

Blake sped off in search of Angela. She leaned against her locker. Heather and Jesse. Married. Finally. And Blake was getting his family. It was turning into a pretty fine day.

CHAPTER 26

Evelyn looked up to see Rob slip onto one of the barstools at the ice cream counter. He gave her a big smile. "See, I'm back. I know, what a surprise, right?"

"So surprising… you haven't been in here in so long."

"I know. It's been twenty-four whole hours."

She loved their teasing banter and really enjoyed their afternoon ritual of taking an ice cream break. She got malts for both of them, and they went to sit at a table by the window while Melody took over the ice cream counter.

"So, I have some news." She looked over at Rob, who paused in devouring his ice cream. "Big news."

"Don't keep me in suspense." He put down his spoon.

"Heather and Jesse are getting married." She was so happy for her daughter. Pleased about the wedding. She could hardly wait to see her daughter marry Jesse. Happiness for Heather squeezed at her heart.

"That is good news. Congratulations."

"They are getting married on Jesse's boat, The Destiny."

"That sounds nice."

She rubbed her hands along her pants leg and before she could change her mind, before she could decide if this was a good idea, she took a deep breath. "I was wondering... I mean, if you're still going to be here in four weeks... Would you like to be my date to the wedding?"

His eyes widened. "Your date-date. Like official date?"

"Yes, my official date. Although I'll be busy with wedding things. I'm planning the food, but Jesse's cook will make it and we'll have servers to deal with it. And I'm walking Heather down the aisle."

"You are? That's wonderful."

"Heather can't decide if she wants to invite Darren or not. I told her it was up to her. He's pretty much disowned her for years, but he is her father. So, I told her I'd be okay with whatever she decides. But she's definite on not wanting him to give her away." She was rambling. She knew it. Was he going to answer her? She took a deep breath. "So… are you still going to be here? Do you want to go to the wedding with me?"

A wide grin spread across his features and reached his eyes, sparkling with anticipation. "Yes, I'll still be here in Moonbeam. And yes, I'll go to the wedding with you."

She wasn't sure if relief or apprehension coursed through her. She had asked him on a date. An official one. Everyone they knew would see them together. Was she ready for that?

"So, I have this great idea." Rob looked over at her expectantly.

"And what would that great idea be?"

"That we should go on some trial dates in the next few weeks. You know, just so our first big date isn't at the wedding with all the emotions and stress that comes with weddings. What do you say to that?"

She smiled. "I think that sounds like a sensible idea."

"How does tomorrow night sound?"

"It sounds like a date." What had she gotten herself into? *Was she ready for this?*

And as he went back to eating his ice cream, she realized... yes, she was ready. And even looking forward to it.

Rob sat a desk in the sunroom of the owner's cottage, the late afternoon sun streaming through the windows, surrounding him. He sat with his laptop open before him, pounding on the keys. His new story poured through his fingers, the writer's block finally behind him. He loved this feeling of being totally immersed in a story. The characters talking to him, surprising him. Times like this he loved being an author.

Violet startled him when she came into the room. "Hey, are you *writing*?" Her voice was full of surprise.

"As a matter of fact, I am. How do you feel about having a writer in residence for a while?"

"Are you kidding me? I'd love for you to stay."

He laughed. "Because I'll be around to help with the repairs?"

Her face grew serious. "No… because I've kind of gotten used to having you around. I like having family here in Moonbeam."

He liked the feeling of being around family, too. Really liked it. Even if Vi could be a pain at time, he adored his baby sister. "Well, I have an actual date with Evelyn to her daughter's wedding. That's four weeks away. So I know I'll stay that long."

Violet grinned knowingly. "Smart woman. Ask you to go to something four weeks out. That gives you more time to get adjusted to the idea of moving here…"

He admitted that idea had run through his mind a time or two or twelve. There was nothing holding him back in Vermont. His lease was up soon on his place back home. Though, Vermont never had really felt like home to him. And Moonbeam sure had better weather than Vermont this time of year. And Violet was here.

And Evelyn.

Just look at all the reasons to move here. But that was silly. He was only just getting to know Evelyn. That should enter into his decision. They hadn't even had an official date yet.

He also admitted that Moonbeam had

grown on him. The small-town charm. The friendly people. Even the gossipy Jenkins twins. Life here fascinated him. Even gave him his idea for his new book.

"And… it appears we're going to be dating some before that. You know, just so we can perfect the dating thing and not have our first date be to a wedding," he added nonchalantly.

"Good plan." She grinned as she sank onto the chair beside him. "So… you're really considering staying here? Like for a long time? Permanently even?"

"You know what, sis? I am."

"Well, that's pretty perfect as far as I'm concerned." She leaned over and glanced at his computer screen. "You writing another thriller?"

"I am. This one is set at the beach. At a small resort. With bright, colorful cottages. In an enchanting small town."

"Good choice." She laughed. "Just don't kill off the resort owner."

"I make no promises," he teased.

"Anyway, you should probably stay here and do more research. About life at an adorable beach resort and all." She stood up and gave his shoulder a playful shove before she left the room.

Research. That was just another thing he could add to his list of reasons to stay in Moonbeam. Not that he needed much convincing.

CHAPTER 27

Evelyn went over to Sunrise Village to see her mother and surprise her with a framed copy of the photo she'd taken at their last Parker women brunch. She hoped her mother would like it.

Her mother answered when she knocked. "Evelyn, it's good to see you."

Much better than the greetings she used to get that usually involved a frown and a why-are-you-here.

"Hi, Mother. I brought you something." She held out the gift.

"Come in. A present?"

She stepped inside and her mother carefully unwrapped the present, looked at it for a long moment, then held it to her chest. "The picture from our brunch. Thank you, Evelyn. This is so thoughtful." Her mother walked across the room and set it prominently on a shelf. The only family photo in sight.

"I'm glad you like it."

"How are things coming along for Heather's wedding?"

"Really good. Just putting the finishing touches on the details."

"That's good."

"You're bringing Ted, aren't you?"

A smile crept across her mother's face that made her look years younger. "I am."

"You've been seeing a lot of him."

"I have. He's… a nice man. He treats me well. He's not… critical all the time."

"You mean like Father was?"

"Yes, your father was a hard man to live with." Her mother turned to glance over at the photo before continuing. "And sometimes I feel responsible for your choice in marrying Darren. Darren was just like your father. You saw your father treat me like that. Controlling. Critical. You didn't think anything when Darren treated you the same. But I think we've both come to realize that we don't have to live like that."

She stared at her mother, surprise sweeping

through her. This had to be the most honest thoughts her mother had ever shared with her. "It's kind of freeing to be out from under that control, isn't it?"

"It is," her mother agreed. "I know I was a bit... judgmental when Darren said he was divorcing you. I insisted you try to fix things. But you know? You shouldn't have to live with a man like Darren. No one should."

"Well, Lacey is. Hope she's enjoying that." She grinned in spite of herself.

Her mother actually cracked a grin, too. "She deserves what she deserves."

As long as her mother was being frank... "So, I've asked Rob Bentley to be my date to Heather's wedding."

"So it was more than a date when we ran into you at the wharf."

"No..." She shrugged. "I don't know. It's all kind of new and confusing. We have gone out to dinner twice more now. We didn't want our first real date to be at the wedding."

"I would imagine a wedding could be awkward for a first date."

And since their newfound honesty was going this well... "Ted makes you happy, doesn't he, Mom?"

Her mother's eyes twinkled with delight. "He does. Very much so. I'm glad... I'm glad we found each other again."

"I'm glad you did, too."

"We have a date tonight."

She was pretty sure her mother had a date with Ted almost every night if the town gossip from the Jenkins twins was right... and they were usually one hundred percent correct in their gossip. "I hope you have a wonderful time."

The faintest blush settled on her cheeks. "Oh, I think we will."

Evelyn left her mother's suite and headed back to the cafe, stunned at the conversation they'd just had. Could it be possible after all these years that she and her mother might become close? Actually become friends?

That was more than she'd ever hoped for from her mother. Honesty. Support instead of judgment. A delighted happiness spread through her. She could get used to this new relationship with her mother. Very used to it.

Patricia waited in her suite for Ted to show up. They were going to go over to Belle Island for dinner at Magic Cafe. Dining outside had never really been her thing, but Ted loved it. And she had gotten a bit used to it... possibly even enjoyed it. The views were really pretty at the restaurants on the wharf. Magic Cafe was right on the beach, and they were timing it so they'd catch the sunset there.

She picked up the wedding invitation sitting on the table. Heather and Jesse. It was a lot to take in. First finding out Heather had a son, and now this wedding. The wedding was scheduled a bit quick, but then she'd never been able to convince *any* of the girls to do things the proper way. And maybe the proper way wasn't so important after all. Maybe. She'd at least managed to keep her thoughts about how quickly the wedding was being planned from Evelyn when her daughter had stopped by today.

She glanced over at the framed photograph on the shelf. The Parker women. Warmth spread through her as she looked at her family.

She did feel like she'd mellowed a bit since dating Ted, with his easygoing ways and the joy he took in even the simple little things in life.

Like when they'd found an out-of-print book at the antique store. One he'd read as a boy. And he was so pleased. Or the first day the new hibiscus plants in the courtyard at Sunrise had bloomed. He'd snapped pictures with his phone and sent them to Cassandra.

And the way he was about Cassandra. Totally supportive of her. Adored her. He was always so proud of her work with finding homes for the foster children. He even seemed to be okay with Cassandra and Delbert Hamilton's budding relationship. Whatever their relationship was exactly. But what future did they have when they lived thousands of miles apart? She kept those thoughts to herself. And really, what business was it of hers?

She put the invitation down and frowned. It wasn't her business what Cassandra and Delbert did. Or the fact that Heather was rushing into her wedding. Why had she always thought that people would want her opinion about what they did with their own life? She walked over and stared at herself in the mirror. How had she become so judgmental? Too much time around her husband, she guessed. Nelson was the most judgmental person she had ever met. Of others. Of her. A strict sense of what was right and proper. Evelyn was right. It was freeing to be out from under that.

The woman in the mirror stared back at her. The woman with wrinkles beside her eyes and the corners of her mouth. She'd aged, but she hoped she'd done it gracefully. She still kept her regular appointment with her hairdresser, and no one would ever see a stray strand of gray hair. She took pride in putting on her makeup every morning. Her nails were done on schedule. So she hadn't totally changed. Not too much.

Then she looked down at her sensible walking shoes. Something she'd never have believed she would ever wear. But they were ridiculously comfortable. And practical for all the walking they did around town. And they were more sensible for going to a restaurant on the beach than her fancy pumps. Someone really did need to design a more fashionable walking shoe, though.

She sighed. She'd become a paradox. Never really certain which person she was. The lighthearted woman she was with Ted. Or the critical woman whose persona was so easy to slip back into when she wasn't looking.

But, she admitted to the woman in the

mirror, she liked the woman she was when she was with Ted. The woman who was easing her way back into her family.

She opened the door to Ted's knock, and he beamed at her. "Hello, there. You look exceptionally beautiful tonight."

His compliments always sounded so sincere. "Thank you." He looked pretty handsome himself in pressed slacks, collared shirt, and casual leather loafers.

"You all set to go?"

"I am." She started to reach for her purse and paused, uncertain if she should say what she was thinking. "Ted?"

"What?" He paused and looked at her.

"I— I'm really enjoying dating you." The words spilled out.

His smile grew even wider, making his eyes twinkle in delight. "And you, my dear, are the bright spot of my life these days." He leaned over and kissed her gently. "I'm so glad we found each other again."

"I am, too." She grabbed her purse, surprised at how she'd just blurted out her feelings about dating him. Since when did she talk about feelings? Well, she had this afternoon with Evelyn, too.

"Let's go. Haven't been to Magic Cafe in forever. I bet we have a wonderful evening." Ted took her elbow and led her out the door.

She bet they did, too. She always had a wonderful time with Ted, and it was a delightful and unexpected change in her life. Like becoming part of the Parker women and their brunches. Who knew a person could change this much, this late in life? Not that she was old, of course. Age was a number, not some kind of life sentence. And in the last few months, she'd felt younger than she had in years.

"You look very handsome tonight, Ted."

He smiled back in appreciation. "Thank you."

Maybe she'd even learn to give out compliments that truly sounded like she meant them. And she did mean that one. He looked positively dashing.

CHAPTER 28

Heather's wedding day came quicker than she could have imagined. She stood poised on the upper deck of The Destiny. The music began to play, drifting across the light breeze as they slipped through the waters of Moonbeam Bay. She peeked around the floral screen at the back of the deck that hid her from Jesse. Livy stood on one side of the pastor, and Blake stood next to Jesse. Jesse looked breathtakingly handsome. Her heart soared.

"Are you ready?" her mother asked as she adjusted the teal ribbon around the waist of her wedding dress.

Grace's wedding dress. The connection wrapped around her like a familiar song, a favorite blanket. She was part of a long family tradition.

She nodded. "I'm so ready."

They stepped out from behind the floral screen and Jesse's eyes locked with hers. Time froze. No one else was there in the moment. She was certain she saw tears in the corners of his eyes.

"Okay," she finally said to her mother, and they walked down the aisle. Jesse took her hands in his when she got to the arbor.

Livy sent her a teary smile, and Blake beamed at her.

The pastor said a few words, and they repeated their vows. Promising to love each other forever, which wouldn't be a difficult request for her. Life might still throw problems their way, but she was sure they could overcome them together. They always had. They always would.

"You may kiss your bride."

Jesse leaned over and kissed her, holding her tight, before releasing her.

"I present to you, Heather and Jesse Brown."

Everyone started cheering, and Jesse took her hand and squeezed it. She looked over at

Blake and reached for his hand. The three of them walked back down the aisle together.

They reached the back of the deck, and Blake turned to them. "Well, I guess this is as good a time as any to ask this question." He turned to Jesse. "Do you think... do you think I could call you Dad?"

A hint of tears clouded Jesse's eyes and the widest grin she'd ever seen spread across his face. "You bet. Yes. That would be great."

A twinge of jealousy swept through her. She should be happy for them. For Jesse. He'd done so much for Blake. Given him a home.

Blake swiveled and turned to her. "And do you think I could call you Mom?"

Her heart erupted in fireworks and tears streamed down her cheeks. She crossed the distance to Blake and took him in her arms, holding him tightly. "Yes. Of course. That would be just... perfect."

Jesse came over and wrapped his arms around both of them. The three of them stood like that, all of them crying. But that was okay. She had finally found her family.

～

Livy dashed away her tears and followed Jesse, Heather, and Blake down the aisle strewn with flower petals. They had timed everything perfectly as the brilliant sunset exploded around them.

She stood there in surprise as Blake asked to call them Mom and Dad. And now the tears fell yet again. At long last, her cousin had found what she always had wanted. A family of her own.

Austin walked up beside her and handed her a handkerchief. "It was a beautiful wedding."

She took the handkerchief and dried her eyes. "It was. Just beautiful." She turned and tugged on his shirtfront. "And next fall we'll have our own wedding. I'm sure glad I have more time than this to plan ours. Not that this wedding isn't wonderful. And Heather got everything just like she wanted. But wow, it's a lot of work to pull off a wedding this quickly."

Austin swallowed and looked at her warily. "About that. I wanted to wait until after Heather's wedding to ask. And I *hate* to ask you this, but it's really important."

"What? You can ask me anything."

"My sister called. She said Mom is still holding her own. But she's not getting any of her strength back. The doctors aren't making any promises. Things could change at any moment." He grabbed her hands. "I hate to do it… But there's something I *need* to ask you. I know we said we'd get married next fall… but… there's no guarantee my mom will make it until then. Do you think… Is it possible… Can we move up the wedding?"

Her heart broke at his news of his mother. She squeezed his hands. "Of course we can. Having your mother at the wedding is important. Marrying you is what matters to me, not the actual wedding. We'll have it as soon as possible."

Relief swept over Austin's face. "Really? You're okay with that? I just can't… I can't imagine getting married without her there."

"And you won't have to. I promise."

Evelyn stood next to the railing with Rob, enjoying the last of the sunset. "It was a wonderful wedding, wasn't it? And Heather looked beautiful."

"She did." He squeezed her hand. "And yes, the wedding was wonderful."

Heather, Blake, and Jesse walked up to them. "Mom, thanks for all you did helping me pull this off so quickly."

"You know I loved every minute of it." Her heart soared at seeing her daughter so happy.

"And I have something to ask you, Evelyn." Blake stood in front of her. "So, you see... I'm calling these two Mom and Dad now." He motioned to Heather and Jesse. "So... do you think I could call you Grams? Like Emily calls Donna?"

Tears started to roll down her face, and she rushed forward and pulled Blake into a hug. "Of course you can. I'd love for you to call me Grams."

Emily walked up to them. "So, what's with all the tears? The wedding is over, you know."

"Emily, I'd like you to meet... Mom and Dad. And Grams," Blake said with exaggerated formalness.

"Well, it's about time." Emily elbowed Blake. "Guys. They can be so slow sometimes. Good job, cuz."

Heather and Jesse went to go talk to some other wedding guests, and Emily and Blake headed off to get something to drink. She turned to Rob and dashed away the last of her tears. "I'm so incredibly happy right now."

"So would it make you any happier if I told you I've decided to stay in Moonbeam for a bit longer? Like quite a bit. Maybe even permanently a bit." His eyes glistened with anticipation of her answer.

She reached up and touched his cheek. "Yes, I do believe you've topped off my happiness quota for the day. I'm very glad you're staying in Moonbeam."

"Do you think we could top it off with a kiss?" He reached out to touch her cheek, and they stood there, connected in the moonlight.

"I think that would be a wonderful idea." She held her breath. Their first kiss. And she knew she was ready for it. So ready.

He leaned in and pressed his lips to hers gently, then deepened the kiss. A rush of pure happiness swept through her. The future looked bright for all the Parker women in Moonbeam Bay.

EPILOGUE

The Parker women sat having brunch the very next weekend. Heather poured mimosas and they sat with notebooks, making plans for Livy's wedding. There was one major hurdle. They hadn't been able to score a venue yet. The Destiny was booked, and it would be hard for Austin's mother to get up to the upper deck anyway. The Cabot was booked, both the ballroom and the pavilion.

"We've got to think of somewhere." Evelyn frowned. "The cafe is too crowded. The gazebo at the park is already reserved for the next four weeks."

"Well, we have to come up with something, because I told Austin to plan on it being in three weeks from now. We really need to have it before his mother takes a turn for the worse. I don't care about anything except Austin having his mom here. We offered to have it at his home, but she insisted it be here in Moonbeam. She's anxious to see the town and where we'll live." Olivia felt tears threaten, and she struggled to keep them at bay. "She has to be here."

Patricia leaned forward. "I'm not really one for outside weddings, but Evelyn, didn't I hear you talking about a new resort opening up in town? Rob's sister's resort? You said the grand opening was in four weeks. Maybe they could hold the wedding the weekend before they open?"

Olivia's mouth dropped open. "Grandmother, that's a great idea. I was over there the other day and they've got the courtyard all redone. It's so pretty. We could rent a tent for some shade."

"Let me call Rob." Evelyn stood, pulled out her phone, and walked to the far end of the lanai.

They all watched as she talked for a bit. Then she turned to them, a wide smile on her face, and gave them the thumbs up.

"Oh, I'm so relieved." Olivia let out her breath.

Evelyn walked back over and sat at the table. "Never doubt the power of the Parker women."

"Okay, so… who is going to be in charge of the flowers?" Heather laughed and grabbed her notebook.

"I am." Emily raised her hand. "I know what Mom likes."

"Perfect. Evelyn has the food, of course," Olivia added and turned to Heather. "Did you get Grace's wedding dress dry cleaned? Because I really, really want to wear it."

"I did. Luckily we're both the same size so it should fit perfectly."

"Not sure I'm going with the teal ribbon and shoes, though." She laughed.

"Hey, put your own spin on it. You'll look beautiful." Heather jotted down notes, ever the organizer.

"I'll say this. I think we are going to pull off the perfect wedding in record time." Donna smiled at all of them.

"Of course we can pull off another wedding. We're the Parker women. We can do anything." Evelyn raised her glass.

"To Livy and Austin. And a perfect wedding at Blue Heron Cottages," Heather said as she raised her glass to Donna's.

Olivia looked at her family, so willing to make this happen for her, for Austin. She was one lucky woman. She raised her glass. "To the best family I could ever hope for."

Dear Reader,

I hope you enjoyed Grace Parker's Peach Pie. Are you ready to find out what happens in book six, The Perks of Being a Parker? Links to all retailers are listed on my website.

kaycorrell.com/perks/

Order it now to find out what happens next to the Parker women. And just wait until you see what Camille is up to! Will this finally be the last of her?

As always, thanks for reading my books. I truly appreciate each and every one of you!

Kay

COMFORT CROSSING ~ THE SERIES

The Shop on Main - Book One

The Memory Box - Book Two

The Christmas Cottage - A Holiday Novella
(Book 2.5)

The Letter - Book Three

The Christmas Scarf - A Holiday Novella (Book 3.5)

The Magnolia Cafe - Book Four

The Unexpected Wedding - Book Five

The Wedding in the Grove (crossover short story
between series - Josephine and Paul from The
Letter.)

LIGHTHOUSE POINT ~ THE SERIES

Wish Upon a Shell - Book One

Wedding on the Beach - Book Two

Love at the Lighthouse - Book Three

Cottage near the Point - Book Four

Return to the Island - Book Five

Bungalow by the Bay - Book Six

CHARMING INN ~ Return to Lighthouse Point

One Simple Wish - Book One

Two of a Kind - Book Two

Three Little Things - Book Three

Four Short Weeks - Book Four

Five Years or So - Book Five

Six Hours Away - Book Six

Charming Christmas - Book Seven

SWEET RIVER ~ THE SERIES

A Dream to Believe in - Book One

A Memory to Cherish - Book Two

A Song to Remember - Book Three

A Time to Forgive - Book Four

A Summer of Secrets - Book Five

A Moment in the Moonlight - Book Six

MOONBEAM BAY ~ THE SERIES

The Parker Women - Book One

The Parker Cafe - Book Two

A Heather Parker Original - Book Three

The Parker Family Secret - Book Four

Grace Parker's Peach Pie - Book Five

The Perks of Being a Parker - Book Six

INDIGO BAY ~ Save by getting Kay's complete collection of stories previously published separately in the multi-author Indigo Bay series. The three stories are all interconnected.

Sweet Days by the Bay

Or buy them separately:

Sweet Sunrise - Book Three

Sweet Holiday Memories - A short holiday story

Sweet Starlight - Book Nine

ABOUT THE AUTHOR

Kay writes sweet, heartwarming stories that are a cross between women's fiction and contemporary romance. She is known for her charming small towns, quirky townsfolk, and enduring strong friendships between the women in her books.

Kay lives in the Midwest of the U.S. and can often be found out and about with her camera, taking a myriad of photographs which she likes to incorporate into her book covers. When not lost in her writing or photography, she can be found spending time with her ever-supportive husband, knitting, or playing with her puppies —two cavaliers and one naughty but adorable Australian shepherd. Kay and her husband also love to travel. When it comes to vacation time, she is torn between a nice trip to the beach or the mountains—but the mountains only get considered in the summer—she swears she's allergic to snow.

Learn more about Kay and her books at
kaycorrell.com

While you're there, sign up for her newsletter to
hear about new releases, sales, and giveaways.

WHERE TO FIND ME:
kaycorrell.com
authorcontact@kaycorrell.com

Join my Facebook Reader Group. We have lots
of fun and you'll hear about sales and new
releases first!
www.facebook.com/groups/KayCorrell/

I love to hear from my readers. Feel free to
contact me at authorcontact@kaycorrell.com

- facebook.com/KayCorrellAuthor
- instagram.com/kaycorrell
- pinterest.com/kaycorrellauthor
- amazon.com/author/kaycorrell
- bookbub.com/authors/kay-correll